MW01167465

KISS IN THE WIND

DANIELLE STEWART

RANDOM ACTS PUBLISHING

ISBN-13: 978-1508805557

ISBN-10: 1508805555

❀ Created with Vellum

KISS IN THE WIND

Looking back can seem daunting. Moving forward can seem impossible.

With an old friend back in her life, will Betty hold on to yesterday even if it tears her apart?

The past can't be rewritten, but the world can be changed—especially if Betty and her family in Edenville have anything to do with it.

PROLOGUE

I've never been able to say no to my wife. It's been a blessing over the years because, usually, everything she's convinced me to do has made my life indisputably better. But this time Alma got it wrong. So if I knew she was wrong, why did I agree with her? It was impossible to argue with the soft blink of her coal-black eyes when her time remaining on this planet was so short. A deathbed promise is a binding agreement and a heavy burden.

When, on one of her final days before she succumbed to cancer, Alma told me she needed me to go back to Edenville, I literally lost my balance. It was as if her words knocked my world off its axis. There was no denying her pleading as the words slipped from her lips, punctuated by a hard-fought struggle for breath. I held her frail hand in mine and swore I would do as she wished. I'd return to the place where she had rescued me. Now I'm here, even if I don't understand why. Because I love my wife, I've slid recklessly back into the belly of the beast I've been trying to keep at bay for over forty years.

I don't know what she wants from me. I'm not Simpson Grafton anymore. I haven't been for a very long time. I'm S

McKinney to anyone who ever asks. And far more than just my last name has changed over the years.

Staring up at the spinning ceiling fan, I try to manage my anger. Every time I wrangle and slam it into submission another thought springs off in a new direction. Like trying to shove an octopus into a duffle bag, I'm finding it impossible to get every facet of my feelings under control.

Overwhelming joy flooded me when I hugged Betty and saw how her life had turned out. Crisp resentment bit at the back of my throat when I realized Edenville smelled exactly the same as the day I left it. A balmy mix of plowed earth and livestock.

I don't want to be here. Not in this tiny room that used to belong to a teenage girl. Not in this town that used to belong to bigots. Maybe it still does. It's like returning to a recurring dream you had as a child. The kind that made you sweat and pant in fear. Remember how your heart thudded and your mouth went dry? Now, what if that place you envisioned was real? What if it existed and was as haunted with ghosts as you remembered? Then, imagine the one person you loved more than yourself had begged you to go there. Would you? How long could you last?

Rolling to my side, I drop my arm over my eyes, blocking out the glow of that damn moon. It's always been bright here. Blame it on the lack of tall buildings and busy streets. The stars have nothing to compete with, but I do wish someone would extinguish them all tonight. Snuff out their cheery shimmering. I want to slip into the darkness. I want the world around me to go so black I have to feel my way around, until Alma's hand reaches out and takes mine. I want to be wherever she is. I don't want to live without her. Because this doesn't feel like living anyway.

CHAPTER 1

"I'm starting to think you're a vampire," Betty teased as she handed Simpson another glass of Scotch. He could sense her reluctance to handing it over. He hadn't been much of a drinker over the years, but once Alma took sick he found it to be a solace he couldn't resist. In the last four days in Edenville he'd wiped out most of Betty's supply, but she'd yet to lecture him on it. He was certain it was coming, but she'd managed to hold back so far. Not an easy task for Betty.

"The sunlight won't kill me, I just don't care to see much of it," Simpson replied as he leaned against the railing of the porch and looked out over the quiet night. In his military career he'd been stationed in dozens of secluded places. But they were never this kind of quiet. The jungles always chirped and rumbled with life. The beaches always roared with rhythmic waves. The midday markets were always flooded with the shouts of competing voices. But here, out on this porch, there was true quiet. It was stifling.

"Peaceful out here," Betty sighed, seeming to read Simpson's mind. "You remember how it used to be out at Winnie's, don't you? We'd sit for hours and just listen to the birds through the windows, trying to figure out what kind they were just by the sounds they made. I loved that."

"If you utter the words *the good old days* I'm not sure I'll be able to take it. Nothing about those days was good. You can remember it with as much sunshine as you like, but I don't remember it that way." There was a nip in his voice he didn't bother hiding. He'd been polite since he'd arrived last week, but every day that passed wore away at that veneer, leaving just his prickly and exposed nerves.

"It's easy to look back and see the past different than it was. Maybe I'm trying to keep it a little rosy, but that's better than trying to pretend we never had any joy. I still remember the way you used to stick those pencils in your mouth and make that walrus sound just to make Alma and me bust out laughing. You were always trying to make sure we were having fun. Even when times were tough." Betty busied herself around the porch, straightening the furniture and fluffing the pillows on the porch swing.

"I think I'll skip dinner tonight. I'm still jet-lagged. I'll just get some rest." Simpson took a long swig from his glass and let the heat run down his throat.

"Why don't you just go?" Betty asked, her voice getting sharper as she folded her arms over her chest. "You don't want to be here, right? So then go. I can't stop you."

"I promised Alma I'd come here. I promised I'd stay and try." Simpson dropped his head in defeat.

"Well you're already breaking half that promise. You sure haven't tried too much of anything since you got here. So why bother? Just grab your bag and catch a flight to some solitary little nowhere. Drink yourself to death. You're already walking around here like a ghost, why not make it official?" Betty grabbed the bottle and topped off his glass with an attitude far from an accommodating hostess.

"I promised her I'd try, but for the life of me I have no idea what that even means. What am I supposed to be trying to do? I just want to be wherever she is."

"You can't," Betty retorted flatly.

"I'd like nothing better than to be honest with you," Simpson sighed wearily. "I didn't want to come here. I didn't want to come back to a place that never wanted me in the first place. But you know as well as I do you don't mean it when you tell me to go." He eyed her doubtfully and watched her stern face soften.

"I'd tackle you and tie you up like a rodeo calf before you could get off the porch," Betty admitted. Simpson couldn't fight the chuckle, and they both broke into a laugh.

"I'm sorry I'm being cranky," Simpson apologized, tilting his head up at his old friend. "I'm all twisted up right now. I'm falling and just trying to figure out how to get my feet back on the ground."

"Well, you could try to be happy. Try to find something here that makes you feel better. Edenville has changed. I promise you it has. But if you can't find a way to cheer up, at least stay busy. Everyone is going to be pulling in for dinner in a little while, and Clay is finishing up at the restaurant. Come in the kitchen and peel some potatoes." Betty took the glass from his hand and placed it on the small table next to him. "Maybe leave the booze before you pickle your insides."

"I don't know how you do it every week. All these people showing up, making a ruckus, and eating all your food. Don't you ever feel like it's too much? Like your house has been invaded?" Simpson opened the screen door for Betty to step inside.

"It's never too much. As a matter of fact, I'm not sure what I'd do if they ever stopped coming. You know better than most how lonely my life was growing up. Having this much family around is the only thing that keeps me sane some days. I hate a

5

quiet house." Betty handed Simpson a potato peeler and pushed the trash can toward him.

"Do you do the potatoes the way Winnie did?" Simpson asked, trying to mask his hopefulness.

"Is there any other way?" Betty smiled. "I have all her recipes written down, but I hardly need to look at them anymore. They're etched on my brain."

"Can you make that pineapple thing she used to make? You remember the one with that cream and the puffy pastry? Alma tried a few times after Winnie died, but she could never get it quite right." Simpson stared down at the potatoes as he peeled them, trying not to think too deeply about the past. He couldn't dive into the pool of his memories where Winnie and Alma lived. He'd never resurface. Every now and then he could dip a toe in, but anything more would be dangerous.

"I sure can," Betty beamed. "It's on the menu at our restaurant. Stop by there tomorrow night, and I'll get you some. You haven't even seen it yet. Clay and I worked very hard getting it up and running."

"Maybe," Simpson shrugged, hating to lie to Betty. He really didn't have any intention of going into town. He'd practically kept his eyes closed on the cab ride from the airport. He didn't want to see how it had changed and evolved. It was easier if he could picture it as the same old awful place. It didn't matter to him if the signs on the storefronts didn't read white only anymore or the water fountains weren't still a source of tension. Edenville could dress itself up anyway it wanted to; in his eyes it would always be the place where evil was allowed to reign.

The squeak of the screen door saved Simpson from having to commit fully to Betty's request. Thundering feet trampled through the kitchen as Betty's daughter, Jules, and granddaughter, Frankie, stepped in. Simpson put down the potatoes and hopped to his feet to take the car seat from Jules's hand. The little baby staring up at him yawned so big he couldn't help but smile.

"Someone looks sleepy," Simpson said as he tickled the baby under his chin. Placing the car seat on the floor, he unbuckled the straps on the seat and lifted Ian into his arms. It had been a long time since he'd held a baby, but once he'd learned that special way to cradle one in the crook of his arm, it was impossible to forget.

"Someone accidently wound his clock the wrong way," Jules said as she started digging through the diaper bag. "He's nocturnal."

"My oldest boy was like that. I was deployed for most of his baby years, but I do remember how hard it was for Alma." He felt everyone's eyes on him as he swayed back and forth gently. He knew they'd all been dying to hear more about his life, and they were hanging on to every syllable he uttered about it.

"If he's holding your baby," Betty cut in, "then you need to be peeling the potatoes. You're early. Dinner is barely started."

"I know," Jules said apologetically. "I was just going nuts in the house. Colic is kicking my butt. I'll help with dinner, but Ian's not really sleeping unless someone is holding him. He cried the whole way to the bus stop to wait for Frankie."

"I told you, have the bus drop her off here for a while. Clay and I can take turns at the restaurant and be here in the afternoon." Betty handed her daughter an apron and a salad bowl.

"He's out cold," Simpson whispered as tiny snores escaped from the baby in his arms. "I can rock with him for a little while if you want."

"Are you sure?" Jules asked, her face lighting hopefully.

"I missed a lot of time with my boys when they were this little. Alma was amazing; I was more the backup than anything. She had the hardest job anyone could ever have. When I did come home on leave, the only thing I was ever good at was rocking the boys. I think I can handle this."

"Thanks." Jules breathed out in relief. "You just have to hold him kind of upright; that seems to help with the colic. Frankie, why don't you grab your book bag and quietly do your homework in the living room while Simpson takes care of Ian."

Frankie nodded and her short bobbed hair danced along. A talkative little girl was not as welcomed company as a quiet little baby. If Simpson had learned anything over the years, it was that little girls could almost never stay quiet, especially when they were told to.

He settled into the squeaky rocking chair and adjusted baby Ian until they were both comfortable. Frankie arranged her books on the small coffee table and took a pencil out of her pink, jeweled utensil case.

"Why didn't you change your first name?" she asked, flashing her curious eyes up at him. She didn't break her stare like most people would with the silence that filled the room.

"I thought you were supposed to be doing your homework," Simpson finally retorted, but still the little imp of a girl didn't blink. She wanted an answer and had no problem having a staring contest until she got it.

"I was just thinking, if you wanted a fresh start why not change your whole name? It's not really that great of a name anyway." Frankie flattened her book out and waited for an answer.

"Most people call me S, so I did kind of change my first name. But if you must know, Alma asked me not to," Simpson offered flatly. "She said she couldn't imagine living with me and calling me anything else. We agreed that anytime we thought it might cause us a problem out in public, she'd just call me S. So that's what we did."

Frankie pursed her lips and made a small noise as if that was a good enough answer. Flipping her notebook open to a blank sheet, she quietly began working. Simpson wanted to pretend he was asleep, or in some way preoccupied, but he had to admit he was fascinated by this child. She resembled a young Betty in so many impossible to ignore ways. Everything from her tiny mannerisms to her big curiosity made him nostalgic. And while most times that unsettled him, this felt different. Oddly hopeful and comforted, like he was back in the presence of friends.

After an hour or so of silent rocking, Simpson's mind unknotted and began to settle, just in time for the dinner crowd to roll in. He was still trying to remember everyone's names and faces. He'd read all the letters Betty had sent over the years to Alma. He knew so many details about their lives, but face to face he had a hard time keeping them straight. Alma would have been great at that. Whenever they went anywhere together she'd prep him and make sure he was up to speed on everyone who might be there. He used to find it tiresome, but now he missed it dearly.

He remembered the best he could. The cop was Bobby. He seemed like a real sturdy guy with his head on straight. He was like a son to Betty since he moved next door years ago. His wife was Piper, an interesting specimen of a woman. She was the type of person who could look at you and see to your core. Her eyes held secrets. Her heart held bruises. He remembered the stories Betty told Alma all about her checkered past. It was no surprise she still held a little pain even if things were better for her now. They had two children, clearly adopted, which was easy to remember as their skin was much closer to the color of Alma's than either of their parents. Simpson liked that about them. An interracial family can be a challenging vehicle to steer, and they'd chosen to take that on.

Clay was Betty's second husband. A nice guy, as best Simpson could tell. Nothing seemed to rattle him much and, judging by the way he looked at Betty, there was a real love

9

between them. That puzzled him though. He could never see a day in his life where he'd find another love after Alma. He was happy Betty had been able to find love after the loss of Stan, but he didn't believe that was out there for him.

Jules was Betty's daughter, mother of baby Ian and nosy Frankie. Jules was the spitting image of her late father, Stan, and he found it hard at times to look at her straight on. Sadness would fill the corners of his heart when he thought of Stan and his other little brothers he'd left behind. Regret was a powerful beast, and when life got quiet you could hear it growling. It wasn't the girl's fault she made him miss his brother, but it didn't make it hurt any less.

Jules's husband, Michael, was a lawyer. And he fit that bill perfectly. Rolling in with a crisp suit and a recently untethered tie hanging low around his neck, he looked wrung out from a long day. Simpson had to admit they were all nice. They popped in to check on him, sent cookies, and stuck their nose in—all in the name of kindness. It was hard to be distant when they kept acting so generous toward him.

"Come in and eat," Betty called to everyone. "Frankie, bring that baby swing in so poor Simpson can have his arms back long enough to get some food."

The commotion was clearly not bothering anyone but Simpson as they all clamored to settle in. Little jokes passed among them all, elbows good-humoredly nudging into ribs as they teased each other. It was heartwarming, but it was also deafening.

"You should recognize plenty of these dishes tonight, Simpson," Betty sang as she scooped a heaping bowl of squash onto his plate.

"It's been such a long time," Simpson admitted as the scent of cinnamon turned his senses into portals to the past. "When Alma was diagnosed she swore it wouldn't change her, but chemotherapy has a way of zapping energy. She didn't cook much after she started treatment. And heaven knows I could never even boil water."

"Is anyone around tomorrow to eat at the restaurant?" Betty asked, and Simpson nervously felt the hair on the back of his neck stand up "I'll let Megan know how many we have coming. She's such a good hostess she gets cross with me if I just show up unannounced with the whole hungry pack.

"I might be," Piper said, pulling out her phone and checking her calendar. "Bobby has a late shift but the twins and I could come. Do you have something special planned?"

"Simpson is coming down for some Pineapple Delight. I was thinking maybe there would be some folks from church who could come by, too. None that would really know who you are Simpson, most are too young, but they're a kind bunch."

"I never said I was going tomorrow," Simpson explained as he stared down at his plate. "You asked, but I never said I would."

"You can't stay locked up here in this house for all of eternity. You've got to go into town and show your face again." Betty's voice was rising and her vegetable-scooping hand was getting firmer as she slopped a heap of squash on Michael's plate. He leaned back in a hurry to dodge the splatter and save his suit.

"I'm not interested in having my life run for me. I can take care of myself and make my own choices. I'm not meaning to sound ungrateful—" Simpson started, but Betty cut in.

"Then try harder, because that's exactly how you're sounding. I'm not going to just let you rot away and not face things."

Simpson could feel his face turning red as he mulled over how to control his temper under pressure. Years of military experience had taught him how to stuff his feelings down, but every day since retirement had made that more and more difficult to do. But just as he opened his mouth, reaching deep inside for diplomacy, there was a knock on the door.

"Wonder who that could be?" Bobby asked as he placed his napkin down on the table and headed to check who it was.

"Surprise guests are always interesting 'round here," Jules said with a smile as she tried to cut the growing tension. Simpson pondered that for a moment, knowing Stan, Jules's father, was always trying to do the same thing when they were young. When their parents fought Stan would try to tell a joke or change the subject. The more he got to know her, the more traits of his brother he recognized in her.

A moment later Bobby returned with a young man in tow. He had shaggy blond hair, a skinny build, and wire rim glasses that kept slipping down his nose. With a leather satchel slung over his shoulder and a crisp white button-up shirt he looked like he had just come from work, though Simpson couldn't make out exactly what profession he was in. But his curiosity was short-lived.

"Ray, what brings you here tonight?" Betty asked, hopping to her feet and reaching out to hug him. "Drop that bagful of papers you need to grade, and stay for dinner," she insisted, but he waved her off.

"It smells delicious, but I don't want to intrude. I just stopped by for a minute to talk. I got held up at the school. I meant to be here before you all would be sitting down to eat. It can wait," Ray apologized as he pushed his glasses up again. "Is Frankie here tonight?" he asked, scanning the room.

Betty nodded. "Our family has gotten so big we can't fit everyone in here anymore. The kids eat in the other room in front of the television."

"I don't think we've met," Ray said as he tipped his head to Simpson. "I'm Ray Archibald. I'm Frankie's teacher."

"I'm a friend of Clay's," Simpson shot back quickly. "The name is S McKinney." Simpson rose and stretched across the table to shake the man's hand.

"It's a pleasure to meet you. Most everyone around here is

Betty's friend. It's good to see they let Clay have some company every now and then." Ray shook his hand firmly. If he found Simpson's alias strange, he didn't show signs of it outwardly. Still, Simpson prayed the anxiety didn't bubble up through his eyes.

"Nice to meet you, too," Simpson lied. He wasn't in the market for new acquaintances, especially in Edenville.

"What did Frankie do this time?" Jules asked, seeming to brace herself for some bad news. She put her fork down and eyed her husband knowingly. "Was she butting in on your teaching again?"

"That's not why I'm here. Well . . . it is . . . but not for the reason I usually am—" Ray stuttered, fidgeting uncomfortably as he tried to explain.

"We've told her a hundred times," Michael cut in, "she isn't to be disrupting class and always interjecting her ideas about things. It's your class she should be there to listen."

"But she was right," Ray countered.

"It doesn't matter if she was right," Michael continued. "We have a rule, and she knows it. You can be right and polite. Those two ideas aren't mutually exclusive. I'll have a talk with her tonight."

"I'm sorry, I'm not being clear," Ray continued, shaking his head. "Frankie wasn't disruptive or rude in any way today. We had some free time after everyone finished a quiz, and she raised her hand. She told me she'd read ahead in her history book and saw we'd be covering civil rights next quarter. She wanted to know why none of the curriculum seemed to talk specifically about local history during that time. I'll be honest; I was caught off guard. It's hard enough getting the kids to read the chapter we're on let alone have them reading ahead and asking questions."

"What did you tell her?" Betty asked, ignoring Ray's insistence that he didn't want to intrude and fixing him a plate to take with him.

"That I'd look into it and get back to her. She didn't like that answer much, but I could tell she was trying not to talk back. I promised I'd have a good answer for her by the end of the week, and that seemed to appease her. The problem is, as you know, I'm not from Edenville. I moved here from California two years ago. You were always so kind to me, Betty. I ate in your restaurant every day for three months until I could learn to cook something for myself. I like Edenville; I think of it as home now, but I'm not familiar with much of its history. I came by tonight to see if I could convince you to help," Ray said hopefully as he took the plate from Betty.

"Me?" Betty asked, placing a delicate hand on her chest. "I'm no teacher. I barely got my own behind out of high school with passing grades."

"But you lived through the Civil Rights Movement. I bet you have stories going all the way back to—" Ray began, but Clay cut him off with a hearty laugh.

"I'd be real careful how far back you go with that sentence. Don't go aging a woman any farther back than she is. It's dangerous."

The group laughed, and the men all grumbled their agreement of that fact. "I meant to say that since I've lived in Edenville I've seen the amazing things you've done for this community. I love teaching here, but keeping the kids engaged is hard. I think they might be even more interested in the lesson plan if it relates to them personally."

"That's the trouble though, isn't it," Simpson cut in, and he felt the table collectively hold their breath. "You said it perfectly there. Maybe not everyone here in Edenville wants to dig up the past and make it quite so personal. You might be getting into something that isn't as welcomed as you think."

Ray twisted his face up as he thought on that for a moment. "We've come so far since then. It was ages ago. I think people can separate the times pretty well. I'm only asking that you think about it, Betty. Help me shape the curriculum. Help me tell the story of Edenville in a way the kids might actually pay attention. It won't be all on you either. I'll do my research. I'm just looking for someone to help fact-check with me."

"I can promise to give it ample thought," Betty said with a smile. "Now, if you are sure I can't make room for you at the table, then at least let me throw a cover on this plate so you can take some home."

"You are too kind." Ray leaned in and took a big whiff of the plate of food she'd made for him. "This will get me through the stack of work I have to do tonight."

Michael filled his glass with water and then spoke. "I am sorry if Frankie has been a handful for you this year. We've heard it from every teacher she has ever had. She means well, but she is still trying to balance having an opinion with having manners."

"You don't need to apologize for her one bit. I'm only sorry she's had teachers in the past who have made you feel like that is a bad thing. Frankie is very bright. She's compassionate to her classmates, and she tends to stick up for those who need it most. Middle school is a battleground these days, and Frankie is a good soldier. Speaking your mind isn't always easy, but she does it with a passionate heart. I think she's remarkable to have such strong opinions at such a young age. It's brilliant."

"Thank you," Jules said through the quiver of tears. Simpson could tell being the mother of a confident child was not as easy as some might think.

"It was good seeing everyone," Ray said, waving goodbye.

Simpson felt a tingle of anger start to grow in him. Why was everyone so dead set on unearthing everything that had happened to him? He wasn't some child's toy that needed to be glued back together. He was a grown man, and he knew what he wanted out of this life. Nothing.

Betty came back a few minutes later and checked the table to make sure everyone had what they needed. "That really does show me how much the world has changed." Betty sighed.

"You might need your rose-colored glasses cleaned," Simpson remarked, and it didn't elicit a laugh from anyone.

"How do you mean, Betty?" Piper asked, trying to defuse the tension.

"Frankie is so much like me when I was young," Betty explained and turned toward Simpson. "You're the only one at this table who can confirm that."

Simpson nodded his head. The resemblance in attitude was uncanny.

"Well then, you'll also agree things you see in her that reminds you of me are the same things that made me a complete outcast. I was compassionate, outspoken, and unafraid. For that I was made to feel less than, unworthy. Frankie is praised for it, as she should be. The world sees people differently now, and I'm glad to know she won't be punished for it the same way I was."

"Every type of injustice that's solved is just replaced by another," Simpson countered. "So outspoken little girls now get praised. That's not the leap forward you're making it out to be."

"You might need to eat some more of my food, because best I can tell you need to get rid of a bad taste in your mouth," Betty shot back with a nip in her voice.

"I need some air," Simpson growled, letting his fork clatter onto the plate and pushing back from the table hurriedly. "I'm going for a walk."

"Wait," Betty called out as he left the room. She was clearly sorry for having a hand in chasing him away. "I'll come with you."

"No," he called over his shoulder as he pushed through the

screen door. He could hear some debate over his shoulder. Michael was insisting Betty stay put, that it was dark now, and she shouldn't be out walking around. Michael demanded a flashlight, and in no time at all, Simpson could feel him at his heels. These people didn't know when to quit.

THE SOUND of chirping crickets and the breeze blowing through the leaves brought him back to days gone by. Stepping into the woods near Betty's driveway, he saw the large boulder that had been there since he was a child. Like falling through a wormhole in time, he found himself face to face with yesterday.

"Tommy," he whispered into the wood. "Tommy don't run. Just wait for me." Climbing up on the boulder, he closed his eyes and was somewhere between a memory and a dream.

"He's gonna find out Simpson," Tommy cried as he crouched down behind the rock. "Just put it back and no one will ever know."

"I'm not putting this book back," Simpson insisted. "It's a list of all the bad things the Klan has ever done. I could turn it over to the police, and they could all go to jail. Or I could tell Daddy I have it, and he best leave us all alone if he doesn't want me to do something with it. Like collateral or something."

Tommy sobbed into his tiny hands. He was small for a seven-year-old, and as the baby of the family he earned the title. Crying was like a second language for him. "He'll kill us," Tommy sobbed out.

"Crybaby," a voice shouted from over Simpson's shoulder. "Giraffe. Where the hell are you two? Something of mine's gone missing, and you're going to tear the house up until we find it." Even if Simpson couldn't recognize the voice, the two cruel nicknames told him it was his father. Simpson had sprouted up quickly, and his gangly legs always made his father think of a giraffe.

"What do we do?" Tommy begged, dropping his head down to his knees in fear. "I don't want him to kill me."

"Run," Simpson commanded as he looked down at the book and then his little brother. "You run until you get to the creek, and I'll come out and get you in a little while."

The rustling of Tommy's shoes had made was enough to draw their father toward Simpson. He crammed the book in a small crevice between two rocks and jammed his hands into his pockets.

"Didn't you hear me calling you, Giraffe?" his father hissed. "You need to get your ass back to the house now. My ledger's gone missing, and no one is going to get a wink of sleep until it's found. Get your scrawny ass back to the house."

"Yes, sir," Simpson said, swallowing hard and bracing himself for whatever hard-handed movement would come from his father. He was right to do so. As soon as Simpson passed by the man he felt the vice-like clamp of his father's hand on the back of his arm.

"That book didn't grow legs and walk away," he growled. "If I find out someone took it there will be blood in the streets tonight. Let me find out it was one of you boys and there'll be bodies swinging from trees. Where is that crybaby little brother of yours? Him not being here right now, that's telling me something. I bet he got his stubby little fingers on it."

"He'd be too dumb to know how to read it." Simpson shrugged, trying to take his brother out of the crosshairs.

"You'd be amazed who's willing to cross you and why. You'd be amazed how little you can trust people. If that boy isn't back at the house, I'll know it's him."

"If it is so important shouldn't you keep better track of it?"

Simpson accused, layering his voice with an attitude he knew his father wouldn't be able to ignore.

"What did you just say to me boy?" he demanded as he spun Simpson around and grabbed his throat. "You are dangerously close to being considered a traitor. All the other boys your age already have hoods, and you just keep finding reasons not to. You're coming to a meeting tonight."

"I can't," Simpson said, clenching his jaw in preparation for the beating he'd be getting. "I have plans. A school thing."

"Bull," his father barked as he cocked his fist back and unloaded on Simpson's cheek. "I heard from your brother you had a little colored girl cornered in the woods, and somehow you lost her the other day. You're a coward and a disgrace, and sooner or later it's going to catch up to you. I'm not going to let you put a black mark on this family's good name. If you want an excuse not to be at a meeting tonight, then I'm about to give you one." With a cascade of his father's fists making impacts all over his body, he tried to shield himself the best he could. But he was no match and wouldn't dare try to fight back. He took his beating. This wasn't the first time. Simpson had learned holding his breath and tightening his stomach helped lessen the pain when there was a blow to his body. It was most important to try to block his face since his nose had already been broken twice, and he worried about looking like a grotesque monster if it happened too many more times.

"You will learn," his father huffed, sounding exhausted by the beating he'd just delivered. "You'll learn, or you'll hang."

He disappeared and left Simpson lying in the grass at the edge of the woods, staring at the stars. There was something so appealing about the distance between the stars and Earth. He wished most days he could live on a star. As he rolled to his side he thought of the ledger and his little brother, two things he still had a responsibility to retrieve from the woods no matter how badly he hurt.

"Simpson," he heard Tommy whisper. "Are you hurt?"

"I told you to run to the creek," Simpson snapped as he tried to get to his feet but couldn't. "I didn't want you to see that."

"He thinks I took the book?" Tommy asked, his quivering chin and wet eyes tugging at Simpson's heart.

"That's why I did that. He'll be too distracted with me to do anything to you. The book is wedged inside that boulder. I want you to come back here tomorrow and get it. Hide it in our secret spot. Keep it for insurance or protection or whatever. Tell Stan you have it but no one else."

"Where are you going?" Tommy cried, clutching at his brother's arm and letting go when Simpson yelped like an injured dog.

"I just have to go." Simpson slipped his hands into his pocket and felt the cold metal of his pocketknife. Stepping into the woods and walking far enough to know Tommy wouldn't see him, he flipped the knife open, running the blade against his wrist deep enough to break the skin. Tonight wasn't his first beating, not by a long shot, but it was within his control to make it his last.

CHAPTER 2

"Simpson." Michael's voice cut into the night as Simpson ran his finger over the scar that was barely noticeable on his wrist anymore.

"I don't want company," Simpson grunted as he quickened his pace farther into the woods.

"You should be well aware by now we don't always get what we want," Michael answered as he ignored Simpson's wishes and met his stride.

"You'd know anything about that?" Simpson laughed sarcastically. "The man with the lovely wife, inquisitive little daughter, and angelically sleeping baby doesn't get what he wants?"

"My wife is, let's just say, high maintenance at times, though I love her. My daughter is a handful, and that baby . . . don't let him fool you for a second, he's allergic to sleeping. I won't lie; my life is great, but that doesn't mean I don't have my eyes open to the world around me. I've worked hard to build what I have. I know you're angry, but you can't just run away." Michael aimed the flashlight ahead of them as Simpson pushed some brush aside.

"You don't know a damn thing," Simpson barked. "No one in that house does. You heard the story Betty told you, and you think you know about me and my life, but you don't. Treat me like a zoo exhibit and a prisoner if you like, but don't tell me how I feel about it."

"No one is keeping you here against your will. You can go any time you like." Michael ducked his head under a low-hanging limb as they pushed farther into the woods.

"Alma is keeping me here. I made her a damn promise, and not a minute ticks by that I don't resent her for making me do it. This place didn't want me forty years ago, and I don't want it now." Simpson looked up at the stars, got his bearings, and then turned left.

"Where are we going?" Michael asked nervously. "I'm not sure walking the woods in the dark is the best idea."

"I did it my whole childhood. My old house is about a mile west. I'm going to see it." Simpson ignored the thickets grabbing at his pants and socks as he moved forward. It was as if they were trying to hold him there, telling him not to go on, but they just weren't strong enough. Much like the people in Betty's house trying to help him.

"For a man trying to run from the past you seem to be heading right for it," Michael pointed out. His know-it-all tone grated on Simpson.

Stopping abruptly and puffing up his chest, Simpson got nose to nose with Michael. "The only thing I've ever run from in my life was this place. I swore to myself I'd never turn tail and hide again. And I never have. Not through a lifetime of service in the military. Not in my marriage. I'm not a coward."

Michael cleared his throat and stepped back, giving Simpson room to breathe. "I wasn't implying you were afraid; I was suggesting you'd given up. There is a difference."

"You bet your ass I've given up," Simpson announced, pushing his hair back in an exhausted gesture. "You know what I want? Give me some quiet island somewhere like one of the places I was stationed over the years. A chair on the beach and as many bottles of gin as it takes to put me to sleep."

"Just sleep?" Michael asked, turning the flashlight toward a noise he heard out in the darkness and intentionally not meeting Simpson's glare.

"My best years are behind me. I cared for Alma for years while she was ill. My wife is gone; my boys are grown with their own lives and military careers. I'm retired. There isn't anything left for me. It's too quiet now, and all I'm left with is time to think. Alma always made me happy and kept me too busy to contemplate all the bad stuff." Simpson didn't turn to keep walking. Instead he kicked some dirt off an old stump and sat down on it.

"I think you answered the question about why she made you come here," Michael offered, still pointing the flashlight into the woods. "I'm guessing Alma knew you pretty well, and she knew you might get weighted down by of all of this once your life got quiet. There's a good chance you've got a couple decades left on this planet whether you like it or not. She didn't want you wasting them. If you give up on yourself on some beach somewhere, you'll be throwing that away."

"And what am I supposed to do here to change any of that?" Simpson asked, genuinely hoping there would be some easy answer. Alma had given him a mission, but no instructions for an end game.

"Maybe she just wanted you to have some people around who cared. Maybe she wanted you to face your demons so they don't sink you."

"How do I do that? I can't just waltz back onto Edenville Town Square and tell everyone who I am. Betty might not want to admit it, but it's more complicated than that." Simpson dropped his head into the palms of his hands and tried to keep his thoughts together.

"No, I don't think you can do that. There are consequences to living under a false identity. But I can start to find some answers for you. I can reach out to some legal friends of mine who are very familiar with the uniform code of military justice. I have another associate in Boston who is retired now but used to work civil rights related cases. Maybe there is some kind of precedence for this."

"And what's all that going to do for me? It doesn't change what I want." Simpson kicked at a rock and frowned.

"You don't strike me as a selfish man," Michael said, finally directing the light back at Simpson. "I know what that's like. You put everyone else's happiness before your own. You wait until you know they are safe and taken care of before you ever think of yourself. Maybe it's the military thing. I know my years in the Marines knocked any bit of self-centeredness out of me."

"I should have known you were a Marine," Simpson scoffed. "You don't have the haircut anymore but that posture just screams jarhead. You have a long line of family in the military, is that why you signed up?" In Simpson's experience many times it was just a sense of belonging that drove people to enlist. They felt some kind of connection to their fathers or their uncles who'd served before them.

"Not even close. I didn't grow up planning to enlist, but I needed a way out of my life and the Corps gave that to me. The G.I. Bill paid my way through school. I can tell just by looking at you that your time, which was much longer than mine, made you into the kind of guy who puts other people's needs first. You always made sure Alma was safe; your boys had every chance they could in life. So let that be the reason you stay." Michael leaned against a tree and tucked one hand into his suit pocket casually.

"No one here needs me. If anything, I'll make their lives more complicated." Simpson's mind spun through what it would be like if people in Edenville knew who he really was. That would not be easy for Betty and her family to deal with.

"Sure they do. My wife cries every Father's Day. Every year on her dad's birthday she has to fight with herself to get out of bed. They still have a cake for him every year. And she looks at you and sees this little glimmer of her dad. You're his brother. You must have stories about him that even Betty wouldn't know. She misses him so much, and the idea of getting to know you brings her hope. My daughter, that little inquisitive imp you were talking about, she sees you as this link to the past. Her whole mind has been split wide open with the story Betty told. It's important to her that you don't just disappear now. And Betty, I don't have to list all the reasons staying matters to her." Michael pulled his phone out of his pocket and silenced the sudden chirping coming from it. That was how technology was these days, always interrupting at the worst time. Another reason Simpson wished he were on an island somewhere, with no cell phone reception.

"I'm not even sure what I'm committing to here." Simpson shrugged, feeling defeated. How could it be he knew what he wanted yet, at the same time, was completely incapable of getting?

"Time. Just commit to a little more time. Let me try to find some answers for you while you give everyone back at that house what they need." Michael was a skilled lawyer, which was becoming very apparent to Simpson. Every time the man opened his mouth he was making a case for something and, to his credit, they were damned good cases.

"I still want to go to my old house," Simpson insisted, feeling like he had to assert himself and stay in control of something. Even if that was only an illusion.

"You know, I do have a car," Michael suggested, fishing his keys out of his pocket and jingling them. "I know you don't want to believe it, but some things in Edenville have changed, including most of this land we're about to walk through. It has houses on it now. I don't tend to trespass on people's property at night in the South, since I'm not bulletproof."

"I don't even know if the house is still standing. My whole family left town decades ago. I have no idea what'll be left there."

"Only one way to find out," Michael said, slapping at a mosquito that buzzed by his face. "Now let's get back to the house before Betty sends out a search party."

"She really can't help herself, can she?" Simpson smirked.

"Nope, she's too busy helping all of us."

CHAPTER 3

"Thanks for coming, Bobby," Michael said as he pulled his car into the driveway of Simpson's childhood home.

"You guys always travel in packs?" Simpson asked, letting the bite in his voice show through. Going back to the house was one thing. He'd agreed to take the car instead of hiking. But inviting more people wasn't part of the plan.

Michael rolled his eyes at Simpson's tone. "I'm a lawyer; I'm good at *getting* us out of trouble. Bobby is a cop; he's better at *keeping* us out of it. I looked up the address online and the property is in foreclosure. It's bank owned, so it's empty, but that doesn't mean we can just stroll up to it in the dark and make ourselves at home. At least if the cops come, we'll have one of them with us."

"This is one of the last houses up here," Bobby interjected, changing the subject. "Most of these have been bought and torn down. People are building huge houses out here since the land is so cheap."

"It looks exactly the same," Simpson grumbled as he eased his way out of the passenger seat of Michael's car. "Busted shutters, a sagging roof, and missing floor boards on the porch. Seven boys can do a number on a tiny house. When we were real small we could get so loud the walls would shake." Simpson stepped up the front stairs and peered into the window. "I hate this place."

"I'm still not sure why we're here then," Michael said, glancing nervously over his shoulder to make sure they were still alone.

Simpson grabbed the flask from his pocket and took a long swig, not bothering to offer it to Bobby or Michael. They had too much concern painted on their faces to indulge. "I want to go in," Simpson declared as he turned the knob that didn't give way.

"It's locked," Bobby said, pointing his flashlight up to the second story windows. "Maybe we can call the bank tomorrow and see if a realtor can let us in."

"I don't want to buy the place; I just want to walk through it. I know how to get in." Simpson moved off the porch with determination. It was still there. The latticework nailed to the side of the house that he'd climbed hundreds of times in his life. "The window over the porch doesn't have a lock."

"You can't be serious," Michael scoffed. "You're not going to scale the side of the house and break in through an upstairs window?"

"That's exactly what I'm going to do." Simpson took one more swig from his flask before tucking it away. Unbuttoning his shirt at the wrists, he rolled the sleeves up to his elbow.

"Bobby," Michael pleaded, gesturing for his friend to intervene, "tell him he can't climb that thing. He's going to fall and break his damn back."

"Do you guys smell that?" Bobby asked, seeming to ignore the two men and stepping back on the porch with his flashlight shining inside. "Is that smoke?" Bobby asked.

"I don't smell anything." Simpson twisted his face up in annoyance. "If you're just trying to get me to keep my feet on the ground, don't bother with the games."

"If I smell smoke I'd be obligated to go in and ensure everything is safe," Bobby explained as he pulled a utility tool from his belt and flipped it open. Prying the door open with a creak and then a snap, Bobby waved them in behind him.

"Smoke, huh?" Michael grumbled as he stepped into the dark house. "Well, you're here. Now what?" As he asked, Simpson plowed past him and headed for the stairs with his flashlight leading the way.

"Are we supposed to follow him?" Simpson heard Michael ask Bobby the question. Michael was sounding more aggravated with each minute that passed.

The truth was, Simpson didn't care if they followed him. He didn't care if they thought climbing up the side of the house was a good idea. There was only one thing he wanted, and he had to believe it was still here. Ducking under the low beam that separated the third floor bedrooms, he ran his hand over the carved marks in the wall he and his brothers had used to measure their heights over the years.

Footsteps up the creaky stairs behind him were accompanied by whispers of concern. "I left something here, and I'm hoping to get it back," he explained, trying to calm their fears.

"Your sanity?" Michael joked as he let his flashlight dance across the small empty room. "How in the world did seven boys live in this little house?"

"Not very comfortably. We were like fighting sardines most days, but when you don't know anything else, you don't really think to complain." Simpson dropped down to his knees at the corner of the room and placed his flashlight on the floor. "Can I have that tool you pried open the door with?" He stuck his hand out behind him, not taking his eyes off the old floorboard.

"Why?" Bobby asked, reluctantly handing it over. "I'm already going to have to come back here tomorrow and repair the door. Let's not do any more damage."

Simpson didn't answer as he stuck the tool between the boards and shook one of them free. "I'll be damned," he laughed as the edge of a rusted tin box caught the light of Michael's flashlight beam. Reaching in, he grabbed the box and instinctually held it to his chest like a hug for an old friend.

"What's that?" Michael asked, crouching down now to get a better look at the mystery. "A time capsule?"

Simpson chuckled. "I guess you could call it that. More like an insurance policy. Or so I thought when I was younger." He lifted the lid with some effort, the years sealing it with dust and age. He let his fingers play over the tangle of things that were once treasures and now meant nothing. There was only one thing that mattered in here. When his hand touched the small leather-bound book, he couldn't believe it was still there. Pulling it out, he brushed off the dust that had gathered and stared down at it.

"What's that?" Bobby asked, bending to peer over his shoulder. "A diary?"

"More like a log. It was my father's manifesto of the Klan. They were a very secretive group, of course. Anonymity kept them out of jail, but there still had to be some kind of record of who was a member, how they showed their loyalty, and what their rank was. One night my father dropped this book out in the yard, and my brother Tommy and I snatched it. He assumed he lost it somewhere or someone had stolen it. It was empowering to know I had it, even if I didn't ever plan to do anything with it."

"And do you plan to do anything with it now?" Bobby asked, looking like he was staring at a cop's holy grail. Getting his hands on something like this could help close some cold cases.

"Not really." Simpson dropped the book back into the box next to some old baseball cards and other small boy's treasures. "I just wanted to see if it was still here. I don't want to go chasing ghosts from the past. Best to let sleeping dogs lie."

"Says the man kneeling in his childhood bedroom holding a book from fifty years ago," Michael said smugly.

"You are a real smart ass, you know that?" Simpson groaned as he rocked backward and got himself back to his feet. "If they're about to tear this house down then there is a good chance they'd find this thing. It's better in my hands than someone else's. It doesn't mean I'm digging up the past."

"Can we go now?" Michael asked, peering out the window. If unwanted company appeared they'd have a lot of explaining to do.

"I've got no other business here. No good memories to hang onto from this place. I spent most of my time looking for reasons not to be here." Simpson dusted off the knees of his pants and tucked the box under his arm. Maybe leaving wasn't quite as easy as he made it out to be. If he were alone right now, he'd likely linger for a while and wander the house, digging deep to find the happy memories he'd buried. He might not want to admit it, but they were there somewhere. There were Christmas mornings with his mother's special pancakes. Late nights reading comic books with his little brothers in a blanket fort.

But those thoughts were much harder to conjure up than the loud shouting matches in the living room about the best way to keep the world from changing. The fistfights in the yard were a much more common occurrence as the years went by.

He'd fought many battles in his life, but the war between forgetting and remembering was the one he'd never been able to win. Most days he couldn't even decide which side he was rooting for.

Simpson moved gingerly down the rickety stairs and toward the door. The book had been important to him. He certainly didn't want anyone else finding it, but there was a part of him that was curious. "I've never read it," he announced as they all got into the car. "I've skimmed it; I know vaguely what's written in it, but I never wanted to really find out all the secrets. There would be names of people who coached my baseball team and guys who helped my dad patch the roof. I never wanted to know for sure what they were capable of because once I did, I couldn't pretend anymore."

"Will you read it now?" Bobby asked, clearly still considering the book to be a possible resource for the police department even all these years later.

"Most of these people are dead or moved on. Knowing for sure who did what wouldn't make a difference now. Looking back is a waste of time." Simpson got in the car, rested the book in his lap, and looked down. Something about it felt heavy. Not in weight, but the idea of it being back in his hands was substantial.

CHAPTER 4

Simpson couldn't decide which he liked less, the bustling in Betty's house when it was full of people or the silence when everyone was gone. The afternoons were painfully quiet. Betty and Clay would both be at the restaurant, and since he'd adamantly declined to eat there, she'd put a plate of leftovers in the fridge for him. He'd try to hold out, insist he wasn't hungry, but at some point Betty's impossible-to-turn-down roast chicken would start calling his name.

But dinner wasn't for hours. There was nothing on television, and the radio was pulling all static today. So sitting on the porch swing, he tapped on the cover of the leather bound book he'd dug up from the floorboards the night before. There was hardly any traffic at the end of the long dirt driveway so the squeaking brakes and roaring engine of a school bus drew his attention. The bus lurched forward and pulled away. Holding his breath, he waited, and a moment later his fears became reality. Frankie was bouncing up the driveway, and she looked fueled by an air of determination, a cloud of dust kicking up under her feet.

"Hi, Simpson," she chirped as she hopped up the stairs and dropped her book bag to the porch floor with a thud.

"Nobody is here. Clay and Betty are both at the restaurant," Simpson explained, hoping this would have her bolting into motion, calling her mom for a ride or something.

"I know." She shrugged. "I took a different bus from school today because I wanted to talk to you." She plopped heavily into Betty's rocking chair and stared at him expectantly.

"They just let you get on whatever bus you want?" Simpson asked skeptically.

"They do when I'm coming here. Everyone knows Grammy. Being Betty's granddaughter is sometimes a good thing other times, not so much."

"Do your parents know you're here? Won't your mom be worried when you don't get off the bus at your house?" Sure, he was concerned about that, but really he was just trying to find a way to get rid of this kid.

"I sent her a text when I got on the bus to come here. She told me not to bother you and that I'd be in trouble when I got home, but it was already too late. Plus I heard my dad telling my mom last night he was coming here after work to talk to you, so I knew he'd take me home later." She riffled through her messy bag and pulled out a stack of papers.

"You just have it all figured out, don't you?" Simpson asked with wide eyes as he took in the girl's confidence.

"I knew I'd be in trouble, but I also know my mom is exhausted, and she'd have to wake the baby up to come pick me up at the bus stop. So really I was doing her a favor."

"Why can't you just walk home from the bus stop yourself; how far could it be?" Simpson furrowed his brows as he looked at the ever-growing stack of papers Frankie was trying to organize.

"It's not far. Maybe half a mile."

"I used to walk four miles into town when I was your age." Simpson raised an eyebrow at her as though he was challenging her logic.

"I don't know why I'm not allowed to walk by myself. I'm guessing it's because of all the junk on the news. My mom says the world's gone to hell in a handbasket, and she doesn't want me wandering around on my own." Frankie pulled the small table toward her and started laying out papers, giving his line of questioning very little attention.

"I guess," Simpson conceded. The girl was right. Things might be less tense in Edenville than when he was a kid, but the world as a whole was a different kind of dangerous. Back then there were rules, and the rules might have been screwed up, but mostly people followed them. Nowadays evil seemed to be more chaotic and random. If he were raising a little girl now, he probably wouldn't let her walking home alone either. "I'm almost afraid to ask what you've got there."

"First, I want to know if you're mad at me about yesterday." Frankie looked up at him with round, angelic eyes, and he felt a pang of guilt for making her worry that she'd angered him. But she snuffed that guilt out in a hurry. "Because if you are mad at me, you shouldn't be."

He chuckled at her candor. "I shouldn't be?"

"No. I'm not dumb. I didn't say anything in class about you or even what happened that night at the school. I know better than to talk about you specifically. But I have a right to try to get my teacher to tell everyone what really happened. It doesn't have to have anything to do with you if you don't want it to." She stared at him, her face flat and devoid of any worry about saying the wrong thing.

"Oh no?" Simpson asked, astonished by the path the conversation was taking. "Because it seems like it has an awful lot to do with me."

"What would it have to do with a guy named S? Just some guy who's a friend of Grandpa Clay?" Frankie grabbed a pencil out of her bag and jotted down a note as though she had hardly any time to talk to him at all.

He had to choke back another chuckle. This child was something else. "I think I must have a curse on me or something. I've got nosy little girls always trying to get me to do what I don't want to do."

"I'm not asking you to do anything," Frankie said, her poker face faltering as the corners of her mouth rose up in a smile. Whatever veil she had tried to pull down over her true intentions had just blown away.

"Sure you're not." He grinned back at her. "So are you going to tell me what you've got there, or am I going to have to start guessing?"

"I asked to be excused from recess today and spent the time in the library. I was printing off some old newspaper articles. We only have one computer in there, so I knew if I didn't do it at recess I wouldn't be able to. You'll never believe what I found," Frankie exclaimed, glowing with excitement. "Read this." She shoved an old article into his hand and pulled her chair in closer. Before he could even get past the headline, she was talking. "This article says the Klan was protecting the town that night at the school. Some garbage about how students rioted, and if not for the brave men in hoods, the whole town could have been burned to the ground. How could they possibly get away with printing that? They called the people who died *criminals*."

"It's not that hard to believe. They'd have needed a story to keep anyone from getting prosecuted. A lifelong supporter of segregation owned the main newspaper. Everything ever printed was slanted that way." Simpson swatted at the paper with the back of his hand and tossed it down, not needing to read it to know it was garbage.

"But why didn't the people who were there that night tell their side of the story?" Frankie spoke like she had a streak of unsatis-fied politician in her blood.

"I don't know; I was busy trying not to die." There was prob-ably a kinder, kid friendly way to have this conversation, but Frankie wasn't acting much like a kid. These were big topics she was trying to tackle, and it wasn't his job to soften it up for her.

"Aren't you mad as hell?" Frankie asked, passing a stack of printed papers over to him. "Don't you want people to know the truth?"

"I'm not sure anyone would want you cursing," Simpson said, as the realization of her passion for the topic became painfully evident. Up until this point he'd thought of her as precocious or impishly nosy, now he could see this for what it was. This was a fire in her belly, and everything she read or heard about that night in history was like gasoline poured over it.

"I just don't understand," Frankie asserted, tossing her bag back down to the ground, the books thudding against the wood of the porch floor. "It doesn't bother you that this is what people think happened?"

Simpson bit at his lip, unsure of how to answer her. If she were a grown-up he'd have some choice words how it wasn't his job to straighten out all the ignorance of the world. But this was a child; even if her question was large, nothing else about her was. Her twiggy little ankles and freckled cheeks made it impossible for him to raise his voice.

"It bothers me," Simpson answered flatly. "But just because something bothers you, it doesn't mean you know what to do about it."

"So you do nothing?" she asked, clearly not meaning the question in the general sense. It was an accusation. The look in her eyes told him she meant, *won't you do something?*

Before he could answer, a car turned to pull up the driveway.

It was Michael, and never had Simpson been so pleased to see someone pulling up to this house.

"Great," Frankie groaned as if her master plan had been interrupted. She grabbed all the papers and started stuffing them in her bag and then turned to look at him quizzically. "You look like Sprinkles."

"Excuse me?" Simpson asked, assuming this was some kind of slang kids were saying as an insult these days.

"My friend Jill has a bunch of horses. I go there to ride on the weekends sometimes. There is this one horse named Sprinkles. She's the best horse they have for competitions. The only problem is every now and then she gets this look in her eye. Something spooks her, and you can see it before it happens. She bolts. You've got that same look in your eye. I have, like, a hundred questions for you, and I can tell you're going to leave."

As Michael parked the car, Simpson thought it over. He certainly did feel like he'd bolt at any minute. She'd pegged him right. Alma would have loved this girl, he thought with bittersweet realization. She'd have sat out on this porch all day long and answered every question Frankie could dream up. It wasn't fair she never got the chance to indulge grandchildren. To spoil them.

"A hundred questions?" Simpson repeated, half expecting her to present him with a list. When she nodded he shot his hand out to her. "Deal," he said, waiting for her to meet his hand for a shake.

"What do you mean?" Frankie asked, wrinkling up her nose and eyeing him skeptically. "What kind of deal?"

"You get one hundred questions. I'll try to answer them the best I can, and I won't bolt, as you say, until I've answered them all." Simpson looked her dead in the eye as she took his hand and shook this agreement into reality.

"Your mother is pretty upset with you," Michael said sternly as he shut his car door and strolled up to the house with a stack of papers under his arm. Apparently this family enjoyed documentation. "Well, right now she's probably sleeping, but when she wakes up she'll be pretty mad at you."

"I know." Frankie held her head low as she fell back into Betty's rocking chair. "I'll take my punishment when I get home. I'm sure no television for a week."

"Simpson and I have some things to discuss, so you can scoot your butt inside and get something to eat while you enjoy your last little bit of television before I take you home."

"What are you guys going to talk about?" she asked, trying to get a look at the papers he had under his arm. His patience for her seemed endless, but she could tell by the look on his face she'd better not press her luck.

"Fine." She shrugged. "Do either of you want drinks at least?"

"No thanks," Michael said, taking the seat she'd just left. She looked over at Simpson to get his answer, and he shook his head.

"Ninety-nine," he shot back with a victorious grin.

"Ninety-nine what?" she asked, looking at Michael to see if he knew what Simpson meant.

"You asked me a question. Do I want a drink? That means you have ninety-nine questions left."

She slapped her hand down onto her hip and grimaced. "That doesn't count. I didn't mean that kind of question."

"A deal's a deal. Now, you might not want to waste anymore. They'll go pretty fast that way." Simpson leaned back on the porch swing and folded his arms across his chest as Frankie stomped off into the house.

"Do I want to know what that's about?" Michael inquired, raising a suspicious eyebrow.

"We reached an agreement; I'll stay long enough to answer a hundred of her questions. She just didn't think to be more specific in the rules," Simpson explained.

"The lawyer in me likes your strategy, but knowing my daughter, you're the one who's gotten in over your head with that agreement. Now that she knows your game, you're in trouble."

"Something tells me you're right. But you didn't come out here today to warn me about the dangers of a deal with a tiny redheaded devil did you?" The smile slid off Simpson's face as he turned serious.

"I'm afraid not." Michael, much like his daughter just had, laid a stack of papers out on the small table between them. "I reached out to some associates of mine to try to find a solution to your situation. I'm sorry to disappoint you, but I don't think I have one. Everything you've done since the moment you began living under a false identity is either null and void or downright illegal."

Simpson watched as Michael leafed through the clipped together papers, looking for one source of bad news or another. "I wasn't expecting anything different, so don't feel like you need to soften the blow or anything."

"If you'd pursued other channels for legally changing your name, this wouldn't be an issue. But you falsified documents."

"There was a death certificate issued for me in Edenville. I couldn't exactly try to get my name changed when I was dead. And because I loved Alma, and Winnie and Nate, I had to stay dead. It's not your job to fix what it caused anymore than it's my job to explain why I did it." Simpson changed his posture, making his back arrow-straight.

"I'm not looking for an explanation, but I'm not sure you're aware of the gravity of the crimes associated with that choice. Serving in the military under a false identity is a crime, but there is precedent, mostly with illegal immigrants, where this has been bypassed. Many who were caught but had served their country nobly were given an honorable discharge and not prosecuted through military channels. It would take letters from commanding officers and compiling your military record, but I do think we could have a chance at not tarnishing your career. You would, however, lose all your veteran's benefits and possibly be responsible for paying back any you've received to date. Now, if we look at your civilian life it's far more complicated. You knowingly allowed yourself to be declared dead and for some manner of resources to be used to either investigate or deal with that death. Not stepping forward means you could be charged with conspiracy and fraud. Anything you did under that false identity would be subject to these charges. Every loan you took out, every contract you signed, would be added to the list of crimes. Your marriage—" Michael started to say, but his words were trumped by Simpson's booming voice.

"What about my marriage?" he demanded, daring Michael to speak out against it.

"If," Michael explained, raising his hands disarmingly, "you choose to come forward and expose the secrets you've been keeping, your marriage to Alma would be invalid."

Simpson jumped to his feet and slammed his fist into his palm. "Do you know how damn hard it was for us to marry? Do you know what we went through to even be able to exchange our vows in the first place? How dare you!"

"I'm not the one who broke the law," Michael shot back, not letting Simpson's anger faze him. "All I'm doing is informing you of the legal ramifications of your choice. You didn't have to change your name. You didn't have to buy a fake identity from some guy on a street corner. There were a thousand miles between you and the danger. A crime had been committed against you, and if you'd faced the truth right away through the correct channels none of this would be happening. I just don't get how you made the leap from leaving town to breaking the law."

"I was a teenager for heaven's sake," Simpson yelled back. "I'd just watched people brutally murdered and barely escaped myself. There was no investigation or justice, and everything I'd ever seen in my life told me I couldn't trust anyone with the truth. In the world I grew up in, the cops weren't there to help you if you didn't agree with them. I needed a job. I wanted a new life, a safe one. That's why I changed my name. If I'd given my birth name and social security number it all would have been over. A death certificate had been issued for me. I'd been declared dead. It's hard to get hired when you're dead."

"So you what, made contact with some sleaze who helps people evade their taxes or dodged going through proper channels for citizenship?" Michael scoffed.

"It wasn't some shady guy on a street corner. It was a woman actually, and she helped victims of domestic violence escape their partners when all other legal channels had failed. I was not the first scared person to sit in her living room and discuss the choice I was making. And for the record, it was a damn hard decision for me. I didn't go into it with a clear conscience. So yes, I broke the law. I did it out of fear and ignorance to the problems it might cause me years later. I made a rash decision that got me into this mess. Do you want a point in your column for being correct? Is that how this works?"

"But somewhere along the way, well before now, didn't you think you should tell the truth? The Klan wasn't strong for too many years after your incident. Couldn't you have contacted your brothers or told someone the truth? When it was still fresh in everyone's mind, when the pile of charges wouldn't have been so tall, you could have spoken up. The law isn't perfect, but it can be navigated if you face things in a responsible manner."

"Yes, because to you the law means everything, right? It's perfect and unblemished. All things can be decided through the system. Anti-miscegenation. That mean anything to you?" Simpson felt fire raging through his body. Maybe Michael didn't deserve to be on the receiving end of his anger, but he looked like a guy who could take it, and for now that was what he needed.

"Yes," Michael said, dropping the papers down to the table. "Those were the laws in place prior to 1967 that made interracial marriages illegal."

"Right. All these laws: separate but equal and Jim Crow—those were all upheld for decades, and we were all just meant to live by them. Then one day those laws came before the Supreme Court and were tossed out for the racist, unjust pieces of legislative garbage they were. But somehow in that shuffle, when I was just trying to live and keep the people around me safe, I broke the law. Excuse me if I don't hold the legal system we live under to the same esteem you do. I've seen how flawed it really is."

"Try not to twist an ankle when you step down off your soap box," Michael warned. "I've never said our legal system is without flaws. I don't even begin to defend the defective laws that shaped this country. You want to be mad at someone, fine, I can take it, but it's not going to get us anywhere."

"Betty always made you out to be a pretty nice guy in her letters. I'll be honest; I'm not seeing it." Simpson leveled his voice as he heard Frankie's shuffling feet in the kitchen.

"Likewise. She had some great stuff to say about you, too, and I'm still waiting to see it for myself. I won't take away from what you've been through but—" Michael leaned back and began rocking casually in the chair as Simpson cut through his words.

"But you just want me to dismiss all of it like it never happened. You want me to void my marriage and everything I did while living under a false name." Simpson tossed his head back in exasperation at the ridiculousness of it all.

"No, you stubborn mule," Michael shouted, "I'm telling you to shut your mouth and keep your secrets, because there is no way for any of this to end well if you don't. You will go to jail. You will lose any financial stability you have, and everything you ever did will be called into question. I just want to understand this better. I want to hear from you why you took such a step when, from my perspective, there were other options. It's important to me to try to understand why you didn't ever tell your story."

"By the time I saw the door open to speak up, it wasn't just about me anymore. The FBI had cracked down heavy on the Klan, and my family was weak, diminished by all the hate they had surrounded themselves with. I was strong then, safe because of distance, and perception in the world had changed. People would have had mercy on me then because the Klan had finally been outed and demonized."

"So then what stopped you?" Michael asked with probing and confused eyes.

"I became a father," Simpson said with a little chuckle. "People say it all the time. Becoming a parent changes your life. No one ever really explains it properly though. I can't either, but I know you understand, because you're a dad too. When my first son was born I didn't want him to have the Grafton last name. I didn't want him to ever know what lies were housed in half his DNA. I was determined to give him the best life possible. He was going to have the childhood I never had, the father I never had. I thought it would be easier if he never knew anything about Edenville or my family. I was right about that. It's been better that they don't know."

"You never told your boys the truth?" Michael asked incredulously.

"No," Simpson admitted. "They know the stories I made up and nothing more. I know there will be a day when I tell them the truth, but it's not now. This lie is a burden, I don't need to break pieces off and hand them to my sons to carry. They're half way across the globe, proudly wearing uniforms, and fighting for their country. Now isn't the time to involve them."

"You're probably right about that. You've already put enough people in the crosshairs with this. I think it's best to wait to tell anyone else."

"Who? What are you talking about?" Simpson asked, full of indignation. He'd worked damn hard his whole life to make sure no one else got mixed up in his troubles. It was one of the main reasons he never wanted Betty to come out and spend time with them.

"Corresponding with Betty over the years makes her part of what could be considered a conspiracy. Even though your circum-stances are different, it is as though you faked your own death, and anyone who would have been aware of that could be held responsible as well." Michael's voice was soft now, the person Betty had always described in her letters shining through. "This is complicated, and I don't want to see anyone get in trouble, not even you. It's hard for me to admit, but I don't see a way to help you."

"I appreciate you trying," Simpson said finally, matching Michael's now controlled tone. "I'm sorry I'm on edge about this. If you only knew how difficult it was at times for Alma and me to be together, you'd understand why I'm sensitive about someone saying our marriage wasn't valid. I hear what you're trying to tell me here. I don't have the option of just strolling down Main Street wearing a sandwich-board sign saying who I am."

"No, you certainly don't." Michael shook his head and closed his lips as if he were trying to keep himself from saying more. And Simpson had an idea of what that was.

"And what I should do is just grab my bag and head out of here before I cause anyone any more trouble or get myself found out. Would it be safe to say you agree with that?"

"I wouldn't say that," Michael shot back, fidgeting in his chair.

"The only reason you wouldn't is because you know it's not what Betty wants, but if you were thinking solely about what's best for everyone, you'd tell me to go. I could be on that island where no one gives a damn what my real name is or who I used to be. Tell the truth; you know that's for the best." Simpson's eyes were dancing with delight that he'd converted Michael to his side of the argument. The man was a skilled debater, and to have him as an advocate for his desire to leave would certainly help.

"I'm not under oath here." Michael shrugged. "Maybe it would be good for you to go, but you won't hear me making that case. We both know if you leave here you'll give up on life, and it won't be long until they're sticking you in a box and burying you on that island you're dreaming about. At least here you have some people who care about you while you grieve. There's hope here."

"Who says I want hope?" Simpson asked wearily, rubbing a hand at his aching temple. Apparently Michael wouldn't be so easily swayed.

"I don't mean you have to have hope, these people have it in spades. Being here, even if you can't be the authentic version of who you are like Betty wants, is still better."

"You are a good lawyer." Simpson sighed, throwing his hands up in defeat.

"Unfortunately this family gives me plenty of practice at keeping my skills sharp. We might look pretty tame, but there were plenty of troublemakers here before you. Let their happiness now inspire you. Don't have hope if you don't want to, but don't give up either."

CHAPTER 5

Frankie shoved the bowl of peas toward Simpson and grunted with a raised eyebrow in lieu of asking him if he wanted any.

"Where are your manners?" Jules scolded as she took the peas and asked Simpson properly if he would like some. She shooed her daughter from the table and back toward the other room where the kids were eating.

"It's not her fault," Simpson explained with a laugh, stopping Frankie before she could leave. "I told her I'd answer a hundred questions for her, and in the last week she's accidently wasted seven already just by being courteous."

Frankie nodded that he was correct. "I'm not talking to him again until I work out the rest of the ninety-three questions I have for him."

"At least he's talking to someone," Betty said, turning her nose up toward the sky as though she were highly insulted. "He's been hiding away from me every chance he gets. Still hasn't even stepped a toe into town yet."

"If you're holding your breath for that to happen, you'll turn purple. Why can't you just leave well enough alone already?"

"I am a woman well into my sixties; it's too late in life for me

47

to start minding my own business. Why do you have to be so stubborn about this? You know I won't give up until I get my way."

Everyone snickered and rolled their eyes at the truth in her statement. Everyone except Michael whose eyes darted around nervously.

"Betty," Simpson said sternly, "I've been waiting for everyone to come over tonight before letting you know, but I'm not going to tell people who I really am. I can't. No matter how much you push me, it's not going to happen."

"We'll see about that," Betty shot back with a goading eyebrow. "People here will accept you. I know they will. I was thinking about it the other night. There is hardly anyone here who would really remember those times that well. Just a handful of people are left who are still living or haven't retired to Florida. It's not going to be as big of a deal as you think. It's more about you doing it for you."

"You're wrong," Michael interjected, and every eye around the table spun toward him. "I'm sorry to be the one to have to tell you, but Simpson cannot divulge who he is without serious legal and financial consequences. Long story short, he'd be broke and in jail. His military record could be in jeopardy. It's not worth the fallout. It's my opinion he should remain living under his alias especially if he plans to stay in Edenville any longer."

"Michael," Betty began, looking like she'd just been struck, "you know better than anyone why Simpson needs to face the past. I will not let Alma down again. I failed her a thousand times in our friendship. This was her dying request for me, and I won't accept your answer. There has to be a way. People would under- stand why he changed his name. They'd get past it."

"The banks would get past it? The government?" Simpson countered with more attitude than the situation called for. "Even if no one in Edenville cares, I've got forty years' worth of fraud and lies I'd have to face."

"I don't accept this," Betty said, standing and stepping out of the room. Everyone sat, silently looking back and forth among one another, until Betty marched back to the table. "Here's why," Betty asserted, slamming a letter down next to the bowl of peas. "She told me to make sure you did this. She trusted me to get you through this time. I won't let her down again."

"Again?" Simpson asked, his brows creasing. "When have you ever let her down before? You were her best friend."

"Oh please," Betty pleaded, waving him off with one hand and wiping a rogue tear with the other. "I could never be there for her the way she needed me to be. I know how hard it was for you two. I had Stan, things here in Edenville settled down, and life got easier for us. I wasn't there when she got sick. I wasn't there for anything. She entrusted me with this, and I'm not going to fail her again."

"Wait," Piper cut in before Simpson could gather the right words to tell Betty how crazy she was for thinking that way. "That's not what she's asking you. She says right here she doesn't want Simpson to get into trouble. I don't think she meant he needs to undo the last forty years; she just wants him to be happy and surrounded by people who love him. She doesn't want him drowning in grief and anger."

"And scotch," Bobby mumbled just loud enough for everyone to hear.

Piper shot him a look before continuing. "Maybe there's middle ground here. You said yourself there are very few people in town who would even remember those days, let alone recognize a man they haven't seen for forty years. Maybe he can stay, but not disclose who he is."

No one spoke. Forks clanked against plates as they were laid down; appetites seemed to evaporate under the weight of what they were facing.

"You have never let her down," Simpson said firmly, staring Betty dead in the eye. "You have always been there for her. Those letters saved her on some days. You don't need to fix me in order to pay some debt to her. Our life was hard sometimes, but it was beautiful. Our love was astonishingly complex and layered with the deepest admiration of each other. Don't pity what we had to go through, because we went through it together, and it was worth every bit of hard work."

"That's the first real thing I've heard you say since you got here." Betty sighed, resting her hand on Simpson's shoulder. "I don't want to lose you. Please stay. Whatever changes or arrangements we need to make, I just want you to stay for a bit. I'm afraid if you go now I'll never see you again."

"You wouldn't," Simpson admitted as he stared down at his half-filled plate. "If I go now, I'd be gone. Maybe I'd live for a few years, but the person I am would be gone. I can admit that. Staying here is probably the healthiest thing I can do. I just don't know exactly how I'm supposed to start feeling better. I see what Alma wanted from me. I see why she thought it would be best to be with all of you. I just don't know what to do about it."

Frankie poked her head into the dining room and cleared her throat. "When Grammy felt like that, she told us all about it. She talked until she felt better, right?" she asked, tipping her tiny head up toward her grandmother for backup.

"It did help to talk about it," Betty agreed. "This here is a great group of listeners. They sat through every moment of my story about what it was like for me, you, and Alma growing up."

"I-I haven't talked about those days in forever," Simpson stuttered, his cheeks growing hot with embarrassment. He could feel every eye around the table looking at him.

"You want me to ask you a question?" Frankie asked with a sparkle of excitement in her eyes.

"Ninety-two," Simpson smirked, and winked at her.

"That one doesn't count," Frankie insisted as she stomped her foot and looked to her dad for a ruling.

Michael threw up his hands. "As far as I can tell they all count. You have to be more thoughtful in your questioning. Always watch for loopholes when making a deal with someone."

Frankie let out the telltale huff of frustrated adolescence and leaned against the wall. "Fine," she said, putting her finger up to her lip as if she were giving something lots of thought. "I have a real question for you. The night you left town, how did you get out? Were you afraid? How far did you go?"

"That's three questions," Simpson shot back.

"Great," Frankie said smugly. "Start with those.

CHAPTER 6

Edenville, 1965

"WE NEED TO GO *NOW*, Nate," Winnie pleaded as she frantically stuffed her bag full of items from her kitchen. "Everyone is downtown, telling their stories and lies to the cameras. We can get out now and never look back."

"What about Betty?" Alma cried as she slung her backpack over her shoulders. "We have to go get her, too. We can't leave her here, not after tonight."

"We can't go kidnap a little white girl and leave the state with her," Nate barked back, the bags under his eyes seeming to grow heavier by the second. "Simpson is an adult, and the whole town thinks he's dead. No one will even know he's with us. That's the best we can do."

"How will we get word to Betty?" Simpson asked, shifting an inch to try to find comfort but only coming up with more pain.

"That's not possible," Nate explained, peering out the window to see if anyone was coming. "She has to believe you're dead too. We can't take any chances. If you leave with us now, there is no coming back. We're going, and you're welcome to come, but that means Edenville and everyone in it is gone for good."

"Fine." Simpson nodded as he closed his tired eyes and rested his head against the wall. His body was so battered and bruised that even breathing was painful. And every time a sting shot through him it reminded him what had happened and who had done it. They'd gotten word this morning that his mother and father were telling anyone who would listen how disgusted they were with their son's actions. They would not bury him. They would not mourn him. The last piece of Simpson's body that was intact, his heart, finally broke too. There was nothing left of him that hadn't been destroyed. "I want to go with you."

If you stacked up every bit of fear Simpson had ever had in his life, it wouldn't come close to the edge of the skyscraper of terror he was standing on as they loaded up Nate's rusty old blue truck. The plan was for Nate to lay him down on a blanket in the bed of the truck and stack all their belongings around him. There were only two seats in the front of the truck, so Alma would sit in the bed too, perched on a box with a blanket over her to keep out the winter air. There was no other choice. It was leave in the dead of the night in the frigid temperatures or run a higher risk of being stopped. If Simpson were found alive, if he were found with them, they'd all be killed.

The pain was blinding as Nate lowered him down onto the hard metal bed of the truck and covered him with a wool blanket. Soon every inch of the truck was filled with their things. Simpson was leaving with nothing but the torn up clothes on his back. His favorite coat, his basketball trophies, and his baseball collection would all be left behind.

Bags of clothes and stacked crates of clanking dishes fell in place around him. Spoons and forks were all rattling around in a box by his head. Hastily packed and forcefully crammed in, Simpson was sure half of their things were broken by now. Alma climbed into the back of the truck and squatted down on top of a bag of clothes. Simpson had to turn his head awkwardly to look up and catch her eye. She was sobbing, shivering from the cold, and looked completely exhausted.

"I'm sorry," he whispered up to her. He wanted to reach a hand out to touch even her boot that was planted just inches from his head, but he couldn't. He was packed in too tightly, his body aching too much to do so.

Her lip curled under the weight of sadness, and all she could offer back was a nod of her head, letting him know she'd heard him. As the engine of the truck roared to life, the metal below his body began to clatter and bang when the truck lurched forward. The journey had begun, and Simpson wasn't sure if his body would hold up under the torturous ride, every bump the truck hit felt like a new blow.

Trying to read the stars and the trees, Simpson attempted to decipher when they'd cleared Edenville's city limits. It's not as though the next town over would be any friendlier or that there would be any milder consequences if they were caught there. It was just a relief to know they'd at least gotten that far.

"We're in Aberdale," Alma called out through chattering teeth as though she were reading his mind. She pulled her knit hat down tighter and covered her chin with the blanket.

"You're gonna freeze," Simpson shouted up at her, trying to make sure she heard him over the whipping wind. "Can't you slide down farther?"

She adjusted the bag beneath her, trying to wiggle down lower, but it didn't work. Finally she grabbed the bag and yanked it out from under her until her butt hit the metal of the truck bed, and the bag landed somewhere on top of Simpson. She buried her face in her hands and sobbed some more. Simpson couldn't tell if she was hurt from how hard she'd hit the truck or just overtaken by the cold and the sadness that was beating at her body.

"It's all right," Simpson said, forcing one of his sliced up hands free and reaching for hers. He pulled it down from her face and laced his fingers into hers. "We'll be fine. We're already out of Edenville, and we're not going to stop any time soon."

"I can't believe we just left her," Alma croaked out. "She's all alone."

"She's not," Simpson insisted, trying to look optimistic. "My brother has her. Stan is a good kid, and I told him to watch out for her. He will. Especially if he thinks I'm . . ." Simpson couldn't finish the sentence. It was one thing to pretend to be dead and have his parents disown him, but to live that lie while people like Betty and Stan cried over him made him feel sick.

"We don't even know where we're going." Alma sniffled, squeezing his hand tighter. He'd liked her for a while; she'd liked him even longer. And up until today they'd never held hands besides dancing together in her kitchen. But it was different now; it wasn't sparks flying and butterflies in his stomach. It was just two lost souls holding onto each other so they didn't feel alone.

They drove for hours, and Simpson never let go of Alma's hand, even as she dozed off here and there. She'd startle awake and clutch tighter to his grip. He'd squeeze back, letting her know he was still there, that they were both still all right.

"We'll need gas soon," Simpson figured, trying to adjust his aching body. Whenever Alma looked over at him he'd tuck the grimace away and try to look comfortable, even though it felt as though nails were piercing his entire body. It was the strangest combination of constant radiating pain, flaring like summer lightning cutting through the sky, and moments of dull aches.

"Maybe you can get out when we stop," Alma said, comforting him.

"I shouldn't," Simpson said, shaking his head. "I'm in a lot of pain. I think I should just stay put until we get to where we're going to stay."

Just as he'd suspected, twenty minutes later as the sun began to rise and the first few egg-yolk-colored streaks began to paint the sky, the truck pulled into a gas station. Alma put her blanket over Simpson so he couldn't be seen, and Nate helped her down from the side of the truck.

"Alma, you go on in with your mama and warm up for a few minutes in the station. I'll fill up, and we'll be on our way. Shouldn't hang out here too long." Nate peeked down at Simpson's one exposed eye and nodded. It wasn't as if they could have a long conversation right now, but that small nod meant everything to Simpson. It was Nate's way of saying everything was still all right, and they'd be out of there in no time.

But it didn't quite happen like that. When Alma hopped back into the truck, she was wiping fresh tears off her cheeks and shaking, not from the cold but from fear.

"We aren't welcome here," Alma choked out as she crouched back down and dropped her head low in defeat. "It's not going to be better anywhere. It's never going to be better."

CHAPTER 7

"What happened in the gas station?" Frankie asked as she grabbed a stack of plates from the table. Betty had said she could listen all she wanted as long as she was helping to clear.

"I never asked and none of them ever told me. I just know it was enough to keep us driving until we nearly ran out of gas. And the next time we stopped no one got out but Nate, and he was quick as a bullet from a gun. We drove that truck for days on end just trying to put Edenville in our rearview mirror. I kept thinking this must have been a small taste of what it was like coming over on the Mayflower. I had no room. I was hurting so badly. I only got out a couple times to stretch my body and relieve myself by the side of the road, otherwise I stayed pinned beneath all that stuff just hiding out."

"You ended up in Arizona, right?" Michael asked, adjusting his baby boy onto his other shoulder.

"We did." Simpson didn't explain any further. He closed his lips tight and looked over at Frankie expectantly.

"Fine," she grumbled. "Why did you end up in Arizona?"

"Eighty-nine," he said victoriously. "Nate had pulled his money out of the bank, every bit of their savings, so they had enough to really start a little something wherever we ended up. I'd never seen the desert. None of us had, and when we got to Arizona it just looked so . . ." Simpson thought on the right words for a moment. "It was so blank. So void of anything that reminded us of home. The gas station and diner we stopped at when we crossed the state line sealed the deal." He stopped again, folding his arms over his chest and leaning back in his chair like his story was finished.

"Oh, you're killing me," Frankie said, clearing his plate. "What happened at the diner in Arizona?"

"I was starting to really get bad. My body felt like it was shutting down. Some of my cuts we'd sewn up had split back open, and I was bleeding again. I couldn't lie there anymore. Nate helped me out of the truck, and I tried to stand, but my legs were shaking so badly. A man came up and opened Winnie's car door for her. Nate and I froze for a moment, thinking the worst. But he just tipped his hat and helped her out. Coming around the other side of the truck, he asked what had happened to me. When we didn't answer he slung my other arm up over his shoulder, and he and Nate helped me inside. Everyone in there was so nice. They brought us lunch and fetched a doctor. There were no signs about whites and coloreds anywhere. There was no segregation, not just in law but in practice. No one was the least bit worried why a white kid was traveling around with this black family. By the time we finished our sandwiches, we all knew that was where we'd stay for a while."

"You drove until the hate ran out," Piper said, her hand falling over her heart. "That's incredible; that journey must have been so hard."

"It was. I thought I'd die from the pain at some point."

Piper shook her head. "No, not just that. I mean you left everything you ever knew, and while you loved Nate, Winnie, and Alma, they weren't your family. To be so far away, to leave under such bad circumstances, you must have been hurting so badly."

"I didn't have time to feel that way," Simpson deflected, shrugging it off. "It wasn't long before Nate had some work at a hospital as a janitor, and we were moving into an apartment. The only thing I was thinking about was how quick I could heal and start working myself. I wanted to pull my weight."

"But your younger brothers and Betty, it must have been so hard to not know how they were doing and not be able to let them know you were alive," Jules said as she oozed empathy he wasn't interested in receiving.

"I told you I'd tell you what happened; I didn't say I'd get into how I felt about it. Those are different things altogether. I think that's enough for tonight." Simpson grabbed the platter of leftover roast beef and started carrying it out of the room.

"But I have a lot more questions left," Frankie complained.

"Not tonight, kiddo," Simpson replied, and as she opened her mouth to protest he continued. "Please, Frankie, no more tonight."

This was the line that separated a young child from a growing one. Frankie could have continued her protest, ignored his signals of feeling overwhelmed, and demanded she get her way, but she didn't. Not adult enough to hide the disappointment on her face, but old enough to realize his pleading for a reprieve was genuine.

He'd always liked to keep his mind tidy, and that brief jump to the past felt like someone had climbed inside and ransacked the place.

When he reached the kitchen he placed the tray down on the counter and braced himself against the sink, gripping his hands tightly on the cold steel. He knew damn well this was part of what Alma wanted. She wanted him to share their story, to tell it out loud so he could finally admit he was angry and hurt. And no matter how deep he'd stuffed it away, he couldn't get rid of it.

59

"Are you still mad at me?" Betty asked as she placed a few dishes down into the soapy water in front of him.

"I was never mad at you. I love you." Simpson sighed, tossing his head back and rubbing at his tired eyes. "Things are just hard right now, and it's exhausting. When is my life going to be easy?"

"Maybe when you're dead," Betty joked and started in on the dishes. "Oh, Simpson, life is fluid. It's not all good or all bad; you know that. And don't forget, you get thousands of second chances; they're called tomorrows. It's all right to be scared."

"I am not scared," Simpson shot back, a completely reflexive response. Of course he was scared, but whether in the military or facing adversity in his every day life, he'd become accustomed to ignoring the idea of fear. If you said it enough you could start to believe you weren't afraid.

"Oh, cut the malarkey," Betty scoffed, shooting him a look. "Who wouldn't be scared? You have no idea what to do with your life. You're back in a place that caused so much pain. You lost your wife. It's not going to help to just sit around and keep saying you're fine. None of us believe you anyway."

"I've faced plenty in my life. You know that. Other than leaving Edenville, I've never run from anything, so I wish everyone would stop acting like I'm a coward just because I don't want to talk about every detail of my feelings. I've been brave plenty in my life."

"Yes you've been plenty courageous in your life, Simpson. You've faced war and hate and done it honorably. But sometimes bravery isn't loud and in your face, sometimes it's just quietly deciding you'll keep trying." Simpson could tell Betty intentionally wasn't giving him attention. She was trying to focus on the dishes so her words didn't feel like a lecture.

"You make it sound so easy," Simpson said. "Alma was always better at this stuff than I am. She could forgive so easily. She could rise above anything. That spirit is what kept me from falling down into all this for years. She's what kept me happy. She's gone now, and my happiness went with her."

"I think she knew that," Betty said softly. "That's why she made you promise to come back. She wanted you to try to find new happiness, something else to live for."

"That's not what I want," Simpson countered. "But I'm ready to give into that idea now. Alma was a master at getting what she wanted; I should have figured she'd keep that going."

"So you'll stay?" Betty asked, clearly trying to not look too hopeful. "You've finally stopped being a fool?"

"Finally," Simpson laughed. "I'm not making any promises though."

"You already have," Betty argued, dropping a dish back into the water. "You owe that girl eighty-something more answers. She's not the kind of kid who will just let you off the hook."

"I can tell," Simpson agreed. "She's just as relentless as you were. But you're right. The world is different. Maybe she'll have better luck with her spunk than you did with yours."

"There is something else you can do," Betty said. "You can dry." She threw the towel over to him and smiled.

"Just like the good old days," Simpson chuckled. "I always got stuck drying the dishes at Winnie's house when we were kids."

"I'm just happy to hear you admit some of it was good. I know you've battled a lot in your life, but those days when it was just us, when we laughed until our sides ached, I loved that," Betty reminisced as she turned to face him.

"I haven't thought about the day we left town for many years. It dawned on me, as hard as it was for me to go, it must have been crushing for you to be left behind. To think I was dead," Simpson apologized, dropping his head down remorsefully.

"I thought I'd die," Betty admitted, choking on the emotion in her words. "I thought I'd never take another step, *that all my happiness left with y'all.*" Betty gave him a knowing look as she parroted back the concern he just had about his own happiness leaving with Alma.

"You always know how to teach a lesson, turn things around, and make people see what's right in front of them. Just like Winnie did. You think Frankie will be the same way? I'm wondering if this is her legacy."

"I think she will if she can just stop getting her butt in trouble all the time. It's not easy being so wise and so little at the same time. I'm glad she's taken a shine to you. It'll be good for both of you. I think we tend to forget what a force she can be because we've seen her only as our baby. Maybe the pair of you will make a great team."

"You know what? I think you're right," Simpson said, smiling way too big for the situation. "Frankie, come on in here." Like a puppy that had been waiting to see her leash picked off the hook on the wall, Frankie came barreling around the corner.

"What is it?" she asked hopefully.

"There's another question wasted." Simpson laughed as he tossed a dishtowel over at her. "Your Grammy has decided you and I would make a great team. Let's prove her right. Dry these dishes will you?"

"He's a clever one, child," Betty said with a wry smile. "You've gotta watch him close."

"Oh I will," Frankie said, narrowing her eyes at him. "He doesn't know who he's messing with." She crinkled her nose up at him and tried her best scowl.

"I'm starting to," Simpson admitted, realizing for the first time in a good while he was doing more smiling than frowning. More laughing than crying. More hoping than worrying.

CHAPTER 8

Simpson had to admit remembering the past was hard, but every now and then he'd unearth something he'd been sorry to forget. Frankie had certainly upped her game the following week, and her newest question had him digging deep in his mind to pull out the answer.

Flipping open a small notebook, Frankie cleared her throat, making sure she had everyone's attention. "When did you and Alma finally get together? Like for real, not just liking each other and not saying anything about it. When was it real love?"

"That's a tough one," Simpson explained, leaning back in his rocking chair on the porch and thinking it over. "Love doesn't really happen all at once like people think. There isn't just one moment. I danced with her once in Winnie's kitchen, and I think I knew then." Simpson thought back to that moment with fondness. Holding Alma in his arms, stumbling over her feet, was like waking up on a slow Sunday morning with the sun cutting into the room and heating your face.

"No," Frankie announced, shaking her head. "We already heard that story from Grammy. I'm asking when you were a couple. Official like. When did you get married?"

"That's another tough one," Simpson said, rubbing his chin thoughtfully. "We were a little on-again, off-again for a while. It wasn't smooth in the beginning for us. You all might not believe it, but I was a little stubborn."

The group broke out in mock disbelief and laughter. "I think maybe that's what brings us all together now that I think of it," Piper revealed. "We all have this streak of persistence that doesn't serve us that well, but seems to help the people around us when they need it."

"I can see that," Simpson said, seeing them with new eyes after spending weeks together. The stories in Betty's letters over the years were starting to make sense now. He could see how Michael's wealthy family and weak morals had driven him to be the man he was today. He was a fantastic father, not because he had a great one himself, but because he decided he would be. Jules was exactly how Betty had always described her, from the first letter after Jules was born right up to her last letter about the birth of Jules and Michael's son. Bobby was clearly the man, the police officer, he was destined to be. Following in Stan's footsteps, he was honorable, admirable, and steady. Someone to depend on when everything else seemed to be falling apart. He was another great father, and it sounded like he was a great brother to Jedda, a man Simpson had heard plenty about but had yet to meet since he was in New York with his sister, Willow, fighting crime or something.

But Piper was the most intriguing girl he had met in years. He'd actually pulled out some of Betty's old letters, trying to remember exactly what her story was. He had to be honest, when he read it part of him was horrified. How could one child endure so much? How could one woman make it through with everything stacked against her? It seemed improbable that this woman sitting across from him on the porch with her beautiful children, a successful job as a child advocate, and a lovely disposition, could be the same one Betty had written about. But the reason started to become clear. It was the company she kept that helped her pull through it.

"I guess the moment we were official was when I finally proposed. We'd been in love for years, but I just kept telling myself being together would hurt her in the end. I thought I knew what was better for her. Even though she kept telling me otherwise, I kept fighting it."

∼

Scottsdale, Arizona, 1971

"It won't be long this time," Simpson lied as he buttoned his uniform jacket and looked over himself in the mirror. He fought the urge to glance up and see Alma's reflection behind him. He could lie to her for her own good, but he couldn't look her in the eye when he did it.

"I just don't see why you signed up in the first place. They never would have called you for the draft. They think the real you is dead, and your new name wouldn't have been in the system. I've been without you through all of boot camp. Now you'll be gone for so long. Haven't you heard the horror stories? Vietnam is a nightmare. Men are leaving, and if they survive they aren't coming back the same."

"You can't believe everything you hear on the news, Alma. You and Nate will be fine while I'm gone. You have each other. And you can write to me and Betty the whole time." Simpson felt like a giant pin, popping Alma's balloon of happiness. But better now than down the road when more of her best years had passed her by.

"Why does it always have to be like this, Simpson?" Alma

asked, a recognizable shake in her voice. The kind that always came before tears. "When we first got out here, we didn't get together out of respect for my parents. They were helping both of us so much. We always said once we were both grown and taking care of ourselves we'd start a life together. Then you started working at the printing factory all the way in Tucson because you said it was your best opportunity to make money."

"It was. I never would have been able to accomplish what I have without going there. It was time apart, but it was for our future." Simpson had been crafting this argument for years.

Alma scoffed as she threw her hands up in frustration. "Then you come home and tell me you've enlisted in the Army. Right in the middle of wartime? We were supposed to have started our lives by now."

"And we have," Simpson defended. "I bought us this house. It's perfect. The duplex means Nate can be right next door if you need him. We'll be married before I ship out, I promise." He did mean it, too. He'd done his best to save up money over the last few years. The house was paid for outright. On top of that he'd socked away every dime he could so Alma would have a good start on her own. It broke his heart to think of her alone, but he also knew their life together would be too difficult. It would be better for her to suffer short term than bear the burden of their life together.

"This country has done next to nothing for us," she sighed. "Why would you volunteer for something so dangerous right when we're about to finally have what we want?"

He prayed she wouldn't make him say it. Hell, he wouldn't admit it anyway. Enlisting was his way of making the choice for them. They'd marry, Alma would be entitled to his benefits, and he'd never come back. She'd mourn, she'd hurt, but eventually she'd find someone else to love. Someone who she could love without the weight of the unsettled world following them everywhere. He was doing this not because he didn't want to be with her, but because he loved her enough to stay away.

"Alma, don't think on this so much. Think about the wedding instead. We'll be married. That's something to be happy about." He let his eyes plead with her in that tired way and prayed she'd let this go. Let him go.

"Is it?" Alma asked, turning away from Simpson. "I think I'll go back over to my room and visit with my daddy for a bit. This side of the house is still yours until we're married."

"Don't be like that, Alma," Simpson pleaded, catching her arm gently before she could leave. "Let's do it now." He ran a finger across the mocha skin on her cheek and watched her damp eyes light up.

"Do what?"

"Let's get married. Why not right now? You can move your stuff in here tonight, and we'll be together all week before I need to leave. We can go down to the courthouse."

"How romantic," Alma shot back, rolling her eyes. "Should we pick up a couple strangers along the way to stand up with us?"

"Did you picture some large church wedding with all our friends and family? Because we have none, remember? This place is more tolerant than Edenville, but they still won't be throwing us a parade. You know that. We don't hold hands when we go down to the market. We don't eat out places together. I can't take you to my company Christmas party anymore than you can invite me to your social group's dance night. We're safer here than anywhere we've been before, but we still can't be like everyone else. So why don't we just go down and get married today?"

"I'm not even convinced you want to marry me. If you loved me a fraction of how much I love you, it would be impossible to even think about leaving me. But leaving seems like the only thing you think about doing. If you don't want to spend your life with me I wish you'd just tell me now and save us both the heartache." Alma had forced her tears to stop now, not wanting them to sway him into declaring love out of guilt.

"You're right," Simpson answered sorrowfully. He watched as her face rose in shock, sucking in a breath and holding it. He moved forward and took her hand, though she was reluctant to give it. Dropping down to one knee, he gazed up to her crumpling face and beamed. "You're so right. This should be romantic. You deserve that as much as any woman in the world. More than any other woman, you deserve romance and joy and to be treasured." Pulling her hand to his lips he kissed it gently, smelling the familiar powdery fresh scent that hadn't changed since he'd first met her a decade ago. "You were one of my first real friends. The first to accept me for the person I really am. You were my first love. Life hasn't given us many days in the last ten years to freely love each other out in the world for everyone to see, but I wouldn't trade our love for one that was easy. We can't go out to dinner, and we can't go to the movies, but we can always be the one place I love best. Together is my favorite place to be."

Alma wasn't sobbing. Her shoulders didn't hunch and shake with emotion. Tears trailed down her cheeks, blazing a path down an otherwise stoic face.

"Marry me today," Simpson pleaded, squeezing her hand tighter. "I don't know what our lives will be like. But the idea of you doubting my love is enough to kill me. Because I have never doubted it for a second. I've tried to convince you a thousand times you can do better, be happier, and live easier without me. But I've never tried to convince myself I could do those things without you. Because it would not be true. You are the best I'll ever have. I'm the happiest I'll ever be. Be my wife. Don't make me live another day without giving you my last name, even it's relatively new to us both," he chuckled at the irony of giving away a last name you'd just paid to make your own. "You have everything else of mine—my heart, and my love. Take my name."

"You always think you know what's best for me," Alma started, dropping to her knees so she could meet his stare. "You think I'm not strong enough to face what comes from our love. I'm not foolish enough to think people will accept us, even though it's legal for us to marry. Nor am I foolish enough to believe I could ever find another love like ours in my life. The first day I laid eyes on you I knew I'd love you forever, even if you never loved me back. When I realized you did, I knew I'd spend the rest of my life with you. Even if we have to be apart right now. I'll wait for you. "

"What did Winnie used to tell us about being apart?" Simpson asked, hoping Alma would say it.

"There's always a breeze to carry something between the two of us." Alma sighed, resting her tired cheek into Simpson's hand. "If we're missing each other, just blow a kiss into the wind, and eventually the other will feel it blow past them."

"I'll feel every kiss, no matter how far away I am." Perhaps she thought he meant Vietnam, but really he meant when all of this was over. A part of him would always be with her. He looked down at their hands, her black skin against his white. He saw the sleeve of his military jacket and remembered the solution to all of this. He hadn't lied about a thing. He never doubted his love for her; she was his soul mate. It's why he knew kissing her goodbye and telling her she could do better wouldn't work. He had to put miles between them. A war between them. Marrying her would ensure no matter what befell him in battle she'd be taken care of. He couldn't stop loving her. He couldn't make her stop loving him. The best he could do was leave, taking the choice out of the matter and giving her a chance at happiness.

CHAPTER 9

"I swear if I didn't already know you two spent a happy life together I'd take my shoe off and throw it at your head right now," Jules crowed. "How could you have pulled a stunt like that? You had this woman who adored you, had since she was a little bitty thing, and all you kept doing was leaving? I'd have chained you to the wall and told you to cut the crap."

Simpson chuckled, but thinking back on those days he knew he hadn't been fair to Alma. He was convinced he'd known what was best for her and had hurt her along the way.

"Did she go with you that day and get married?" Frankie asked, not caring if she burned through another of her hundred questions.

"She did," Simpson explained. "It was Nate and a friend of hers from her bridge club that came and stood up with us. Sally something or other—I can't remember her name, but she came only on the condition that Alma didn't tell any of the other girls in the club what she'd done. It wasn't anything fancy but I'll tell you something, it was still one of the best days of my life. Even if I didn't see a forever in my future with Alma, being married to her for a minute would have been better than never being married to her at all."

"I thought things were different out west," Frankie said, looking to her daddy for an answer so it wouldn't count as a question for Simpson.

"Just because interracial marriage had become legal in the late sixties didn't mean it was widely accepted right away. Even out west where segregation was no longer an issue, many folks still thought of marriage as something better kept between individual races. Alma and Simpson could be married, but you wouldn't see them being invited to social events or treated fairly."

"Still," Jules said, narrowing her eyes at Simpson, "how could you keep leaving?"

Simpson shook his head as though he couldn't come up with an answer right away. "I've never loved anyone the way I loved Alma. I cared more about her future than about my broken heart. Or my life. Don't get me wrong, I'm not defending it now. It wasn't long before I realized how wrong I'd been. You asked when were we married, and I told you."

Bobby tossed another log on the fire that burned in the fire pit in the corner of the porch. He'd been quiet each time Simpson spoke about his past and was by far the hardest of the group to read. Maybe that was his police training, to listen and give no personal opinion, but the less he said the more Simpson found himself wondering about Bobby's thoughts on different matters.

"Bobby," Simpson said, offering him a beer from the cooler at his side. He'd tried to ease up on the hard liquor over the last week, but if he ever wanted to sleep he still needed a little help. "Have you ever had to put your feelings aside because you thought you knew what was best for someone?"

"Not the way you're saying," Bobby replied, and Simpson could see a flash of his convictions. "I think it's one thing to walk away from someone for their own good, but that's not what you were doing."

"What do you mean, Uncle Bobby?" Frankie asked, her large eyes innocently beaming above on her cherub cheeks.

"Never mind," Bobby said, grabbing a beer and nodding a thank you. Every adult in the room understood. Everyone here knew this was the second time they'd heard of him dancing with the idea of letting go. Giving up. Trading in his life. Bobby settled back into his chair and tried to avoid his niece's eyes. "You said you changed your mind. What made you?" The tactical change of subject was met with the anxious nods of everyone who seemed to be wondering the same thing.

"My First Sergeant Bill Wilder changed the course of my life. It'd be fair to say without him I wouldn't have had the time I did have with Alma. My boys wouldn't have been born. I owe him a lot."

"How did he finally convince you that you were wrong?" Frankie asked, making an annoyed face at her mother who waved her over for another squirt of bug spray.

"You sure you want to burn through those questions so quickly?" Simpson asked, pulling a small pad from his pocket and making a few more tick marks. He knew it drove Frankie batty, which was the only reason he really did it. Before he could launch into his answer, two headlights came shining up Betty's dirt driveway.

"Isn't that Ray?" Michael asked, craning his neck to get a better look at the small hatchback pulling in.

"I swear I didn't do anything," Frankie insisted, tossing her hands in the air, claiming innocence. "Every time my teacher shows up here doesn't mean I'm in trouble."

"Maybe I am," Betty sighed as she stood up from her rocking chair. "I've been putting him off since the last time he was here. I still haven't given him an answer about helping with that lesson plan he was working on."

"It's not like you to put things off," Clay said, trying to read her face. "You must really be unsure what to do."

"I've been making that difficult," Simpson said, spinning off the top to his beer and taking a swig. "I know if it weren't for me being here you'd be jumping at the chance to help."

"Sorry to intrude again," Ray apologized as he pulled a large file box out of the back of his car. "I swear I'm not just here for leftovers."

"You're here because you're still waiting for an answer from me," Betty said as she gestured for him to come up on the porch.

"I thought maybe you'd caught wind of all the chatter by now," Ray said. "You're usually the first to know everything."

Betty hummed her disagreement. "As a general rule I try to mind my own business."

"Everyone back up," Michael joked, leaning his chair back on two legs. "God's about to shoot some lightning down on this porch."

The rumble of laughter stopped abruptly when Betty pointed a stern finger at him. "God's too busy keeping track of your smart-ass remarks to be worried if I'm stretching the truth. Now Ray, what's in the box? A bribe to help sway me?"

"I wish it were, but I can't think of anything you don't already have. Family, a roof over your head, and a restaurant you love. This box isn't filled with anything but junk, and that's the problem. That's why I'm here." Ray set the box down on the small porch table next to Betty and looked around at everyone in the group. "I bit off more than I can chew, and I'm not sure what to do next."

"You're being a little vague," Michael said, strolling over to the box and looking over the stack of papers. "Whose services are you most in need of? Me the lawyer, Bobby the cop, Piper the self-declared psychologist? We've got a little bit of everything here."

"I need Betty the politician," Ray chuckled. "You see, the last time I left here I dove right in. Meeting with Maryanne, my principal, was first, and she was very interested in my pitch. I told her I wanted to do more than just cover civil rights next quarter; I wanted to show the kids the legacy of Edenville in the process. She was thrilled."

"Guessing she's not from 'round here," Simpson grunted as he tossed a beer up at Ray. Luckily, Ray's quick hands juggled the bottle and got hold of it. He spun off the top and nodded a thank you for it.

"She's from New Hampshire," Ray answered with a knowing look. "So she had a meeting with the school board, and this whole thing grew legs and ran away on me. I'm in over my head and not winning any popularity contests in town all of a sudden. Today I had nine angry parents waiting for me after class. Apparently they've gotten word I'm spearheading this curriculum, and they're upset."

"What would they be upset about?" Frankie asked with an edge of anger in her voice. It was enough to make most of the adults realize it might not be best to involve her in this conversation.

"Frankie, can you go check on the twins please?" Piper asked, softening her face and making it hard for the child to say no.

"I always get kicked out when things start getting interesting," Frankie huffed. She bit at her lip, knowing she was outnumbered and trying to keep herself in check.

"Have a second piece of cake," Betty offered, patting Frankie's back as she slinked into the house, rolling her eyes in frustration.

"The kid had a good question," Simpson said, stopping his chair from rocking and waiting to hear what Ray might have to say about it all. There was a small ember of anxiety burning inside of him, and he figured Ray was about to toss some lighter fluid on it. "What were the parents so upset about?"

"The actual curriculum is their problem," Ray explained. "They wanted details, every detail really, about what I planned to teach. And I couldn't answer because, to be honest, I'm at a loss myself. I don't know how to tell this story. I don't know how to make it something these kids can digest."

"You've taught civil rights before, I'm sure," Piper pointed out. "You taught for a few years before coming to Edenville, right? You must have covered the topic."

"That was different," Ray explained. "I was out in California. You could put some distance between the information and the kids. I covered the laws. Brown vs. the Board of Education is pretty easy when you don't have to look at them and say how profound the verdict was and then turn around and tell them their town ignored the law for years. That when they did finally get forced into integrating their schools it was loaded with hate, bigotry, and violence. Teaching it in that context is entirely different. I wanted to find the heroes of civil rights, the moral victories, but the more I dig the worse it gets."

"And obviously the parents in your classroom today already knew that," Clay interjected, reaching into the box and pulling out a few papers.

"The parents heard what I planned on teaching, and they weren't happy. Some of them were downright furious at the idea of digging up the past. Apparently they'd prefer it if their kids didn't understand how close to home this hit." Ray sank into the chair Frankie had just left and grabbed a handful of papers out of the box.

"What are they afraid of?" Jules asked, sounding agitated. "Kids these days have no shortage of crap to watch on television and danger on the Internet. They honestly don't think their kids are prepared to hear what happened here in their own backyards?"

"They don't want their names brought up," Betty announced as she shook her head, clearly having a sharp sense of the trouble now. "It's not to say they were involved, but maybe their uncles fought for segregation. Maybe their grandmothers stood outside the school and spit on the black kids brave enough to integrate. If you start pulling out photos and articles, it's going to drag their family line through the mud."

"That box is full of it," Ray admitted. "Every single thing I've found about Edenville's history during the Civil Rights Movement is disturbing. But it's also clearly only one side of the story. These articles I found at the library are impossible to believe. They are completely biased and transparently so. There has to be another side of the story. A side these parents wouldn't mind their kids hearing. You asked if I'd taught civil rights before and I have. I've taught about the heroes and the wins. The change that drove this country forward. I still think there is a lesson here that can impact these kids, I just need some help finding it."

"Sounds like you're up the creek," Bobby said, turning his eyes toward Betty.

Nearly everyone on the porch did the same, eyeing her expectantly. She groaned and squeezed a wedge of lemon into her tea. "I suppose you expect me to be the paddle then?"

"I think it's a great idea," interjected Michael, who'd stayed uncharacteristically quiet up until this point. Simpson watched as he locked eyes with Betty in some knowing exchange. "I think you could be a real help," he continued.

After a moment of careful thought as she stirred her spoon in her tall glass of tea, she looked at Michael one more time. "There are plenty of stories worthy of teaching a class, a whole generation for that matter. There are victories. But there are also deep, deep sorrows. Losses beyond measure. There are secrets and murders and grave injustices. There'll be no escaping those facts once you open the door. And no matter how I help you, there will still be folks in this town who will not approve. But I believe in what you're trying to do, and I'll help where I can."

"Talk to them . . ." Ray pleaded, "the parents with concerns. Maybe if you tell them how important this is, they'll listen. Everyone always listens to you."

Betty sighed. "If that were true I'd have had a lot less trouble with this bunch than I did over the years. People don't listen until they're ready to, and I'm not convinced everyone here is ready to listen to everything you've got in that box. Maybe we should just start calling it Pandora."

Clay leaned in and kissed his wife's cheek. "You'll find a way. You've always found a way."

"Why do I always have to?" Betty laced her fingers with Clay's and squeezed his hand tightly.

Bobby was the first to answer her rhetorical question. "Because if you didn't have so many of us stirring up trouble, you'd have nothing to do. Can you imagine just sitting around doing needlepoint and yelling at the television all day? Our nonsense keeps you young."

"If that's true, at this rate I'll live forever."

CHAPTER 10

"You and your family are always stirring the pot, Betty," Krissy Marino accused as she folded her arms across her chest and looked around the packed dining area for support. Betty had called a meeting at her restaurant so she could gauge just how much fight these people had in them. Michael had convinced her it was better to be steering the ship than to be blindsided you. The goal was to keep Simpson's secrets buried, nothing was more important. So at least if she were involved she could have some control over that.

Rolling up her shirtsleeves with great intention, she stared at the stern faces that filled her booths and tables. "Nobody minded when I stirred the pot and got that Bio-whatever company to stop poisoning Clark Creek. Nobody minded when we helped get extra resources here after that storm blew through. You can't expect us to be the pain in someone else's butts when it suits you and not think occasionally *you'll* need to deal with *us*, too. Now, I can understand why you'd be concerned, but you haven't even heard what Ray has to say yet. You just heard civil rights in Edenville and got up in arms. Don't you think maybe that's the problem?"

The grumbling crowd quieted and Norm Richardson, a stocky

pig-faced man who'd never seemed to agree with Betty on anything, spoke up. "You're the problem," he sneered. "You stir ideas in people, and you make them think you know what's best for everyone. I've got two boys in that school. They play on the football team, wearing Edenville's uniforms with pride. This teacher, who ain't even from here, thinks he should come in and make us all ashamed of our heritage. It's a disgrace. Let him teach whatever he wants on the west coast. Not here."

The tone of the group let Betty know most agreed. Looking out among them, she knew none were even around for the worst of it. Either they hadn't lived in town back then or they were too young. "Judging something before we know anything about it . . ." Betty started, pausing so they could all read her accusing glare, "sounds like maybe it's the people in this room who need to hear about the past. Because we haven't come far enough if that's what we're doing these days." Saying *we* was a tactic that had worked magic for years. It was really *them*, not her, but sounding inclusive in your charges against people always seemed to soften the blow.

"Why can't he just use the text books?" Krissy asked, throwing her hands up and trying to get the group to voice their agreement. She was from a long line of Klan members, and though Betty never thought her to be a poisoned well like they were, she certainly had her moments of thick-headedness. Many of the people here tonight were the grandchildren or nieces and nephews of well-known bigots. It didn't mean they were bigots too; it meant they might have been told a different version of history than she'd witnessed. All the more reason to teach it now.

"He can," Betty shrugged. "I mean, you haven't been out of school that long, Krissy. Tell me what did those books say? What do you remember about those lessons? I'm guessing not much, for the simple reason it was just words on paper. We can do more for these kids. We owe them more than that. Something they can remember for a lifetime."

"No one wants to say it?" Norm asked, looking around the room to see if anyone would speak up. "Fine, I will. It's pretty clear why he wants to dive so deeply into this. He has his own agenda, and I don't need my kids dealing with that. Maybe in California it's acceptable, but here we don't need the preaching and the political slant on everything. He's trying to convince our kids that his *lifestyle* is anything other than what it is: an abomination."

"I'm going to do you an enormous favor right now, Norm," Michael cut in, though he had promised he'd bite his tongue and let Betty do the talking. "I'm going to shut you up. Because nothing you can say on that is going to help your case. How Ray lives his private life has nothing to do with this. You can have your own opinion, but don't share it here."

"Oh please, don't make me look like a bigot, the way you're trying to make the families who built this town. Nobody is throwing bricks through the guy's window; no one's threatening him. He can do whatever he wants with his life; I just don't need him tying his beliefs to his lesson plans and forcing it on my kids. Bringing up civil rights now is just his way of preaching to the world he should have the right to marry a man or whatever. It's apples and oranges, and that fruit don't belong in our school."

Betty felt her blood boil with anger. Norm had pissed her off over the years. All the people who'd come through her life needing help—Norm was there to make them feel less than. That was always his game; he only felt big by making someone else feel small. Even better if he could get a crowd to do it with him.

Ray had walked into Betty's restaurant a couple years ago with a look on his face that screamed brokenhearted. She'd assumed some little tart of a girl had done a number on him, so she did her best to cheer him up and make him feel welcome. As they became closer over time, Ray told Betty about the man he'd followed east because of love. And how he'd been brutally disappointed when the relationship fell apart. In that moment, even though Betty hadn't had much experience with it, she could see that a broken heart, no matter the circumstances, hurt everyone the same. People were people. And being hurt by someone you loved stung.

"I can assure you—" Ray said, taking a step away from the wall he was leaning against and placing a hand over his heart as though he were ready to swear whatever he was about to say.

"Don't even," Michael insisted, motioning for Ray to step back against the wall. "You're not going to drag this discussion off topic, Norm. This is about improving the curriculum on a very difficult topic and ensuring our children, mine included, get the full picture. Making it into anything other than that is working an agenda."

"Who the hell made you the voice of morality?" Norm asked, slamming his hand down on the table as he stood. Everyone who was grumbling fell silent. "What you choose your kid to know about the world has nothing to do with how I raise mine. You want to dig up the past and spin the stories? My daddy was there that night at the school. I know you plan to tell that story; I'm sure of it. Four people killed, but you'll turn that into a travesty. My daddy told me how it happened. He told me how the tension hit a boiling point, the violence was imminent, and they did what they had to do to keep their families safe. I have no reason not to believe his story."

"No reason?" Betty asked, perching her hands high on her hips. "How about the fact that it makes absolutely no sense. That there is no proof to support that version of the truth."

"Betty," Clay said softly as he sidled up to her and touched her shoulder gently. "That's not what tonight is about."

"Isn't it though?" Norm asked, stepping forward. "That's what all of this is about. Good and evil, one side has to be completely wrong and the other a bunch of martyrs. That's what you want to tell these kids. You want to take all the grey area out of it and stuff your ideas down their throats."

"I was there that night, and you weren't even born yet," Bettys shouted, her eyes exploding with vehemence. "The only things standing there were good and evil. Fear and hate. Children against grown cowardly men with white hoods. You want to make a case for the other side of that, you can try, but I will stand here all night and tell you the truth. Over and over until you finally understand that the people who died that night were just trying to live their lives, while the people who did the killing were trying to stop them from doing that."

Norm rolled his eyes and threw his hands up dismissively. "Look who all this is coming from. Your daddy had that same hood in his closet, didn't he? He was just as likely to have been there that night, and yet you have no loyalty to him. You want to parade around like you've made this town so much better over the years, but Krissy is right. You and your people just keep making trouble. You bring ex-convicts, liars, and the children of murderers into this town and act as though they deserve every opportunity that the rest of us do. Look at this one," Norm said, gesturing over to Piper. "We all know her story now. She brought a killer to Edenville a decade ago, and we all learned the kind of trash she came from. Now with your help she's in our schools, she's running programs that involve our kids every day. You're like a magnet for the degenerate, and instead of telling them to go you make a place for them here. Now you've got some other guy in your house, and God knows what his story is. Can it actually be worse than hers?" Norm asked, gesturing again at Piper. And with that the dam that held their small but fierce group gave way and the first through was Bobby.

"You have something to say about my wife?" he hissed as he

charged toward Norm and lowered his head so they were eye to eye. Bobby was tall, kept his black hair nearly shaved, and held his shoulders and chin high. Always ready. "You can say it to me. Piper is an advocate for at-risk children. She puts her life on the line some days just to make sure kids get the care they need. You worthless piece of dirt, you don't deserve to breathe the same air as her, let alone insult her."

"She's no different than Betty," Norm continued as he cut the distance between himself and Bobby. "Betty brings in strays and apparently, judging by those kids of yours, so does your wife."

"Oh, hell no," Jules hooted as she plowed forward and nudged a seething Bobby out of the way so she could get at Norm. "You don't speak that way about my niece and nephew. They are my family, and if you have something to say about them, you better do it while running. I will yank out the last few hairs you have on your head and feed them to you." Bobby caught Jules by the arm and held her back from pouncing any farther.

Norm chuckled victoriously. "You see, you made my argument for me. Any disagreement can reach a boiling point, and people can turn toward violence. Look how quickly this escalated. You've proven my case."

"The only thing that proved," Bobby said, loosening his grip on Jules, "is that you are an antagonistic jackass with nothing better to do than cause problems. I'm a police officer trained in keeping my cool in the face of ignorance and provocation. But I'm also a father who will teach you the lesson you need to be taught if you talk about my kids again."

"None of this matters," Krissy interrupted. "I just got an email from the school board. Many of us were in there today, and it seems they agreed with our points. They've changed their mind. They want the curriculum that's provided in the textbooks to be followed. There's nothing else to talk about. It's clear from their message they won't be opening this back up for discussion for the remainder of this school year at least."

"Problem solved," Norm sneered as he grabbed his hat from the rack by the door and pulled it down onto his head. "I knew reason would win out."

The bell over the door chimed as he left, and Betty could see the wind leave the sails of all her family. They'd tucked Simpson and Frankie out in the kitchen, but she was sure they'd been listening, and though she couldn't see the disappointment on Frankie's face, she could almost feel it pouring through the walls.

"He's an ass," Krissy admitted, gesturing toward the door where Norm had just left. "You know better than anyone he just likes to be argumentative. He's got nothing better to do."

Jules, now looking slightly more composed, rested a hand on Bobby's shoulder. "Thank you for not letting me rip Norm to shreds. Why do some people always have to be that way?" she asked, looking over at her mother.

Betty hummed her disapproval of the whole situation. "The devil has better music and some people can't help but dance." The look she threw at Krissy came right back her way.

"Don't stare at me like I betrayed you. Can you hear me out at least first? Norm doesn't speak for everyone here tonight." Krissy stood her ground and insisted on being heard.

Betty grabbed a rag from the counter behind her and started wiping down the table Norm had just left as though she couldn't get rid of his presence fast enough. "If you don't speak for yourselves then the loudest voice does speak for you."

"Well I'm speaking now," Krissy said, touching Betty's shoulder lightly. "Piper is a blessing to this community. She's helped so many children in need. And," Krissy turned to look at both Bobby and Piper, "your children are angels and welcomed with open arms. If I ever saw or heard anyone making them feel otherwise, they'd answer to me. And I know everyone else in here feels the same way." A sea of nodding heads all tried to convince Betty. "You know my family had a heavy hand in the things that happened here," Krissy continued. "My granddad, a few of my uncles—I know who they were in all of it."

"So you're afraid of what people might think?" Betty asked her, palms sweaty with frustration and anger. "The people who died deserved better than to disappear just because the people who lived didn't want to be inconvenienced by the truth of their wrongdoing."

"No," Krissy said, shaking her head. "I am different than they were. My children have been raised differently. But my kids loved their great-granddad. He was a gentler man by the time they came around, and they adored him. I've already been through it with my older boys. They learned all about civil rights in depth in high school, and they came home with questions about where our family stood on it all. But at that age I could explain it better to them. I'm not saying I don't want my younger boys to know about the past and the part our family played in it. All I'm asking is that it's on my terms when my children get told about it. Frankie is a special girl. She's compassionate and an old soul. Not every kid her age is going to be able to understand these topics the way she does. I'm not ready to have a teacher decide when it's right to tell my son who he's from."

"That wasn't my plan," Ray said meekly, still looking rattled by it all. "I wasn't going to make a list of the offenders and start making a family tree of hate crimes or something. I was looking for the heroes. The people the kids could rally behind and root for."

Krissy's face was soft but unwavering. "The problem with that, Ray, is if there were good guys there would have to have been bad guys. The kids will want to know. They'll beg to understand it. I applaud what you're trying to do. Nowadays it's hard to

85

find a teacher who is attempting to energize the students and teach topics in a new way. They're just not ready for it."

Betty straightened the salt and pepper shakers on a few empty tables and turned toward the group. "They aren't, or you aren't?"

Krissy dropped her head as though she'd been caught. "Maybe you're right. But that doesn't change the fact that the school board agrees now. I don't think it belongs in that grade in our school. I want those heroes to be remembered too; I want the good stories told. If you find another way to do that, I'll be the first in line to help."

"I don't agree with you, Krissy," Betty admitted with a sigh. "But I can see your point, and that's maybe as close to common ground as we'll find tonight."

Everyone took the cue and began scrambling to their feet, chattering and nodding goodbyes as they headed out the door in a herd. After a few minutes of clamoring, the place was emptied of everyone but those who'd come in with Betty that night.

Bobby grabbed Piper for a quick hug and whispered something reassuringly in her ear. But she didn't need it. Piper wasn't one of those people who were bruised easily by the words of others. She was the kind of person who didn't have time to care what someone else thought about her.

"I'm sorry it didn't work out, Ray," Betty apologized as she handed him a plate of food she'd wrapped up earlier for him. "I'm sorry for all of it."

"You were always so kind to me from the first day I got here. I was nervous as hell, but you fed me and told me all about yourself, and I felt right at home in your restaurant. You're a good person, Betty. There are a lot of good people in this town. You call most of them family." Ray's eyes welled with a hint of tears, but quickly he composed himself. "Maybe I am in the wrong spot. I can stand here all I want and tell you I wasn't trying to push my own agenda. I wasn't. But maybe I was hoping a lesson about acceptance, bravery, and equality might ring true with someone in my class. And there are plenty of applications for that today. But at least we tried."

"Oh, child, hush up," Betty laughed, slapping his shoulder lightly. "We don't wave the white flag around here, we tie it into a sail and ride out the storm. This thing is far from over. I'm sure of one thing now: for every article of garbage misprinted in this town there should be a story of bravery and kindness. Stop sounding like you've given up."

"But the school board sounded firm in their response," Ray stuttered, looking around the room for some backup. Everyone else knew better than to doubt Betty.

"When one door closes—" Betty started, and when Ray cut in she let him.

"I know, another door opens but—"

"No, when one door closes we go around to the back of the house and jimmy open a window. Then we help boost each other through. I don't think for a second the school board will change their mind. That doesn't mean we can't still do something. Krissy is right, Frankie is an exceptional child. This is important to her, and so it's important for us. Now take that plate and head home. When we have a plan we'll tell you."

The bell over the door jingled again as Ray sulked his way out. Betty was cleaning off a few more tables when she felt two twig-like arms wrap around her.

"Thank you for trying," Frankie said as she squeezed her grandmother tightly. "I'm sure we can think of some other way."

"That is so grown-up of you." Betty spun her body around and rested her arms over Frankie's shoulders. "I thought for sure I'd be wiping tears off those little cheeks of yours."

"I just tried to remember what you told me about things. I don't always get what I want, but there are some people who would love to have what I already have. I know you'll help me figure something out that will be perfect. I believe in you." Frankie tucked her chin down and leaned in for a hug. Betty's heart sang. She realized Frankie was getting older but couldn't help relishing she still smelled like fruity kid shampoo. What a paradox it was to be a growing girl.

Reluctantly letting go, Betty winked and blew Frankie a kiss as she fell into her mother's arms. "You went crazy on that guy, Mom. I thought you were going to deck him."

Jules's cheeks went red as she stuttered over her words. "I don't condone violence but in certain circumstances, I mean when someone is . . ."

"I get it, Mom, don't worry." Frankie let her mother off the hook just as Simpson came out of the back room with two kids over his shoulders like sacks of potatoes.

"These two have more energy than a bucket of possums. I don't know how you keep up with them," Simpson joked as he handed one child over to Piper and one to Bobby.

"Thanks for keeping an eye on them. I'm glad they weren't out here," Bobby said gratefully. Simpson gave a knowing nod and looked over to read Piper's smiling face. She seemed completely unfazed by the insults tossed at her and her children.

"They're perfect," Simpson retorted, making sure she could hear him. "Great kids with great parents."

"So what do we do next?" Frankie asked as she filled a rubber tub with dishes from one of the tables. She'd honed her skills at busing dishes over the last couple of years, and anytime she was at the restaurant she always made herself useful.

Bobby sat his son down at a booth and walked over to Michael and Simpson. "I can talk to my captain. With Betty's statement and maybe that book you have we could reopen this case and bring some more attention to it."

Michael shook his head in disagreement. "The last thing we want is more attention to the actual case. With today's technology and forensics someone will pick up on the fact that Simpson survived. It'll open a can of worms we're trying to avoid. And I don't see the point in naming names when the majority of anyone involved is either dead or moved on. I'm a huge advocate for justice, you know I am, but I don't think chasing down the people involved makes sense. Not now."

"I'm not looking for that," Simpson chimed in. "I don't want anyone getting pulled out of his old folks' home and put in jail. I had my days of wanting revenge and wanting people to pay, but now the only thing we'd be doing is punishing their kids and grandkids with the truth. Even if you could prove who was there that night you'd never know who actually committed the murders. It won't bring anyone back, and I'm with Michael, I don't think it's the right thing to do."

Piper shifted her daughter on her hip and stepped into the conversation. "So what are our goals here? What's everyone looking to accomplish if it's not bringing people to justice?"

Frankie tossed some more silverware into the tub and spoke up. "I want everyone here to remember what happened. I don't think it's right that the people who died that day just disappeared from history. I thought we would learn about it in school and everyone would get a chance to understand it, but that's not going to happen. There has to be some other way to honor them. Some kind way the whole town could support. Maybe a memorial."

"And how about you, Simpson?" Piper asked, drawing Simpson's eyes up from his shoes where they'd settled while Frankie was talking.

He grunted something inaudible and shrugged his shoulders. The silence that came in the wake of his lack of answer was painfully awkward.

"Frankie," Jules said, finally breaking it, "can you take the twins out back and help them clean up their toys. They need to pack up all their stuff."

Looking like a deflated balloon, Frankie nodded and took the twins by the hands. Her hunched shoulders and downturned mouth made Betty want to stop her in her tracks and cheer her up. She was clearly disappointed in Simpson's answer. But she knew Jules had sent Frankie away for a reason, and she always tried to let her daughter do the parenting, even when her instincts told her to jump in.

Jules checked quickly on baby Ian who was still sleeping peacefully in his car seat before marching over toward Simpson. "Sit down," she insisted, pointing at the table to his left. His face went from confused to fearful as she said it again, this time more sternly.

"If I were in your shoes, I'd be feeling exactly the same way. I'd want my ass in the sand somewhere while I got to the bottom of as many bottles of booze as I could. You got dealt a crappy hand here and with losing your wife. If the circumstances were different, I'd probably be in your corner telling everyone that you're a grown man and to give you some space. But you see I have a problem now," Jules said, sitting down across from him.

"And what's that?" Simpson asked, trying not to sound annoyed.

"My daughter cares about you. She's invested in what happens to you. and I don't intend to let her watch you give up. I can't. She's at a place in her life where she believes anything is possible if you try hard enough. She's watching you, and that shrug and grunt you just gave is going to take all the wind out of her sails. That's not going to work for me."

"Listen," Simpson began, both his palms planted firmly on the table. "She's a great kid. I like spending time with her because she reminds me of the time I spent with Betty when we were young. She has this persistence and innocence I've not seen since then. But that doesn't change the fact that I truly don't have an answer to what I want to happen now. Do you know how impossible it feels to have someone make you promise you'll find peace? That's incredibly vague. Alma didn't leave me any clues; she didn't give me any help. You ask what I want to do next, and I have no clue. I can't change the past. I can't undo anything that happened. When that jerk was in here running his mouth I wanted to plow through that door and lay him on his ass. I'm angry and no closer to feeling peaceful than I was when I got here. I don't know how I'm supposed to feel better."

"I don't care," Jules replied flatly. "I don't care if you have to fake it. You said it yourself—Frankie is just like my mother. Look at the woman my mother became even when everything was stacked against her. Look at how many people she's saved even when no one was supporting her. Now imagine for a second the kind of woman Frankie could be with nothing standing in her way. Imagine how far she could go with all of us behind her. You can't change the past, but maybe Frankie is your second chance at it. When my mother was young, you had to tell her to stop, to be quiet, to retreat. You don't have to do that now. You have a chance to inspire, to support, and to encourage. Don't waste that opportunity. Frankie wants to change the world. As her mother I'm not going to let anything stand in her way, and right now your indifference is doing just that."

"Do you honestly think the people who just sat in this room— that jerk who wouldn't shut up—you think they're going to just sit back and let Frankie tackle this? There will be pushback; there will be drama. Why would you want her to go through that?"

"She's going to go through it no matter what she does, because she's the type of person who takes risks and speaks her mind. My job isn't to fight her battles, it's to clean her wounds when she gets home. And luckily, in this day and age that's just a metaphor, we don't have to worry about what y'all did back then. But any type of pushback she gets, any type of trouble that comes of it, she'll know she has all of us by her side. She'll never feel alone. You could be a part of that."

"Aunt Piper," Frankie called as she made her way back toward them with a bag full of toys and the twins in tow. "I think I got everything packed up."

"Thanks sweetheart." Piper smiled, taking the bag and slinging the strap over her arm. "You're such a big help."

"Is everyone going home?" Frankie asked, a slight slump of disappointment still weighing her shoulders down.

Before anyone else could interject, Simpson pulled out the chair next to him and waved her over. "Don't go just yet. You should tell me more about what you're thinking for a memorial. Maybe I can help."

If it were possible to bottle up the burst of joy that played out on Frankie's face, Betty would keep it for all time. Her back shot arrow-straight, her eyes lit with excitement, and her hands clapped together as she slid into the chair next to him and announced, "Just wait until you hear my ideas."

CHAPTER 11

Simpson wasn't opposed to Frankie changing the world. He didn't mind the idea of helping her, and it even kept his mind busy. The problem was talking about the past. It was like pulling out the stitches on a wound that hadn't quite healed yet.

Another little meeting had gathered. There had been a handful over the last few days, and each one made Simpson feel a weird mix of excited and melancholy. Today Bobby, Michael, and Frankie popped in with updates.

"Have you found them yet, Uncle Bobby?" Frankie asked as she plopped heavily down onto the porch swing next to her uncle.

"I have," he replied flatly. "Unfortunately I didn't find much good news. Of the three people who were killed at the school that day I could only find next of kin on one. Mrs. Ellie Perry had two daughters. They were toddlers when she was killed. Her husband died a couple months ago, but I have the phone numbers for her daughters here."

"I'll call them," Frankie said, snatching the paper away. Like a flash, Michael was by her side, stealing the paper from Frankie.

"*I'll* call them," he corrected. "It's not something you just ask outright. I think it's better if an adult calls."

"How could the other two people not have kin?" Frankie asked, turning back toward Bobby. Simpson was still too hung up on the name to be able to process anything else. Ellie Perry was a teacher who, just like Winnie, had begun working at the all-white school under threats that her children would be forced into kindergarten in an integrated school if she didn't take the job. And just like Winnie, she chose to protect her children from that hate. Unfortunately she lost her life by doing so.

Flashbacks washed over him, and he felt the hair on the back of his neck stand up. Ellie had been just feet from him when she fell to the ground. He could still hear the thud of her body against the cold dirt. Two men were already on him, slashing at his skin with the knife they pried from his hand. He couldn't reach her. He couldn't get to her. His helplessness hurt more than anything being done to his body. When he was slammed down to the ground, his face was inches from Ellie Perry's, and he could tell she was dead. Not by the pool of blood under her head but by the lifelessness in her wide open eyes. A few moments later he'd heard someone shout, "Burn their bodies," as the smell of gasoline filled the air.

The fire next to him in the small metal pit on the porch popped and crackled suddenly, and he jumped from his chair, letting it topple down behind him. "Stop," he yelled, throwing his hands up and clenching them into fist. "Don't hurt her," he begged, charging across the porch. "Don't burn her." Michael caught him by the arm before he could pass and spun him around. Simpson, one of the few people who had the height to see nose to nose with Michael, leveraged his force and slammed Michael backward against the wall.

"Bobby, take her inside," Michael demanded as he stared into the Simpson's wild eyes. "I got this, just take her inside."

For once, Frankie knew better than to protest or ask a question. She shook under her uncle's tight grip and inched past Simpson, darting through the screen door and into the house.

"Simpson, it's me, Michael." He raised his hands up disarmingly. "No one is hurting anyone right now. It's just you and me on the porch at Betty's house."

"Betty," Simpson breathed, letting go of Michael and turning quickly to see over his shoulder. "Stan has her, right?"

"Simpson, look around. Look at me. Think about where you are." Michael's voice was calm and steady as he pleaded with Simpson to let reality back in.

"Oh hell," Simpson said, covering his eyes with his hands. "I'm sorry. That hasn't happened in a long time. I just hadn't thought of Ellie in years, and then I remembered what she looked like, what they did to her. The fire, it just reminded me."

"It's no problem," Michael assured him as he reached out and gently touched Simpson's shoulder. "I can't imagine what it was like to be there that day. I'm sure you'll never forget."

"That's the thing, the only way I've made it this far is by forgetting. That's easy to do when you're raising a family and going off to war. It's easy to do when you're so far away and so many years pass, but now, what we're doing, I can't even imagine what my brain is going to remember. I'm not sure I'm ready for that."

"You don't have to be. I know Jules told you she wanted you to be here for Frankie, but there are other ways. You don't have to immerse yourself in that day again. You can help pick the type of memorial that's built or help organize some things. Don't put yourself through this hell."

Simpson braced himself on the porch railing and stared out, trying to catch his breath. "Winnie used to tell us sometimes the only way to get out of hell was to hustle. You can't go over it, you can't turn around and go back, but you can run until you see the light of day again."

"Kind of like pulling the Band-Aid off quick rather than leaving it there to pull a little at a time?" Michael asked, dropping his hand from Simpson's shoulder and standing next to him to look out on the front yard.

"Exactly."

"Everything all right out here?" Bobby asked, stepping back out onto the porch and assessing the situation.

"Peachy," Michael joked. "But for an old man this guy is still pretty tough." Michael rubbed at his shoulder as though it was aching.

"Don't you forget it," Simpson laughed. "I'll be all right. I just got to yank the Band-Aid off and start dealing with this. It's not going away, and maybe I should stop pretending it all never happened. People deserve to know it did. Ellie's daughters deserve to know how brave their mother was. I know things they might want to hear."

"Piper has some contacts," Bobby said meekly at first, clearly uneasy about the offer. "She could get you the number of someone to talk to. It would be confidential."

"Maybe," Simpson shrugged. "I think I'll just start with talking to all of you. If you still want to listen."

Frankie pressed her face to the screen on the door and smiled. "You still never finished telling us what changed your mind about you and Alma."

"I guess I didn't," Simpson retorted. "And I owe you the answers to a lot more questions, too. You got your list ready?"

"Yep," Frankie said proudly. "But if I ask any before everyone else gets back here tonight they'll be mad."

Simpson looked up at the ceiling of the porch and wrung his hands together. "I'm sorry if I scared you," he sighed. "I just got confused."

"You didn't scare me," Frankie replied as she stepped back onto the porch. "If you'd have really gone crazy my daddy would have kicked your butt. Then Uncle Bobby would have arrested you. I don't get scared when they're around."

"You're very lucky," Simpson said, finally looking down at the little girl. "I can't imagine what it would have been like to have an army of people ready to kick butt for me when I was little."

"It's pretty great," she said with a grin, evoking a laugh from everyone on the porch. "But at least now you've got an army. They'd kick butt for you too if you needed it."

"How do you know that?" Simpson asked, the corners of his mouth rising in a curious smile.

"You're family. It's a lot of work to be in this one, but you always know someone is watching out for you. It's why I say how I feel. That's easier to do when you know someone is going to back you up."

"I guess it would be," Simpson replied, looking over at Michael and then Bobby.

"She's right, you know," Bobby grinned. "This isn't always the easiest family to be in, but we are fiercely loyal. We've got your back no matter what."

"I'd like to be there when you call Ellie's daughters. Obviously I can't tell them who I am, but they were so young when it happened. Maybe they'll have some questions, and I can find a way to answer them. Their mother was very brave."

"There's something else I looked up for you," Bobby began, clearing his throat nervously. "I know you haven't had any contact with your family since that day, but I have some information on them if you want it."

Simpson cut his eyes away quickly, biting nervously at his thumbnail as he thought it over. "I know my folks are dead. That didn't happen too long after I left. Betty kept tabs on all my brothers as long as she could, but eventually she lost track of them."

"You don't have to hear it now, I just wanted you to know I have it if you want it."

"I really don't care about any of them except my two youngest brothers," Simpson said firmly. "The rest of them couldn't have cared less about me while I was alive, didn't mourn me when they thought I was dead. But my little brothers, they were good boys. I'd like to know how they're doing."

"Thomas is an engineer in Mississippi. He's got a wife named Ava and two daughters who are in college now. I found them on social media," Bobby explained as he pulled a photo out of his pocket and handed it to Simpson. "They seem really happy."

Simpson clutched the photo between his fingers and turned his back toward Michael, Bobby, and Frankie. His brother looked so different, so bright-eyed and joyful with his arm around his wife and their daughters on either side of them. It took his breath away to see the ease with which Thomas could smile. Simpson used to have to work hard to get his little brother to laugh, considering their circumstances.

"Why didn't Grammy keep in touch with them?" Frankie asked, trying to get a look at the photo in Simpson's hand.

"You'll have to ask her," Simpson replied, turning so she couldn't get a good look at the emotion painting his face. Every minute he'd lost with his brothers had felt like it was stacked up and just dropped on his head. He didn't even know the names of these girls. His nieces. He didn't know anything about his brother except what he loved at the age of nine. "My other brother, Gary, how is he? Did he marry?"

"I'm sorry to say he's dead. He was killed in Vietnam." Bobby's voice was low and calm like he was skilled in delivering bad news. "I couldn't find out much else on him, though his record in the military was exemplary."

"He was always taking a lot of chances. Even when we were kids Gary was brave. I figured he'd have enlisted when he was old enough." Simpson wanted to ask more questions. How Gary had been killed, how old he was. But he knew it wasn't likely to make him feel any better.

"I'm sorry your brother died," Frankie offered quietly.

"They've all been dead to me for over forty years. I don't know any more about them than I do about a stranger on the street. I missed everything. I missed it all."

"Frankie, go on in and grab your book bag and get your homework started," Michael instructed, pointing firmly toward the door.

"You don't have to send her away," Simpson sighed, turning to face them all. "The past is the past. If I could get it back, do it over again, it would mean choosing between the life I had with Alma and having a chance to know my brothers and their family. I'm glad we don't get those kinds of choices."

"It'd be better if you didn't have to make those kinds of choices at all." Frankie stepped toward him, peering at the picture in his hand and leaning her head gently against his arm as she smiled down at the photo. "I wish you could have had it all."

CHAPTER 12

Vietnam, 1972

"GET your ass over here now," Sergeant Wilder shouted through gritted teeth as he pointed a filthy finger at Simpson. He was the epitome of what a commanding officer should be. His voice was like the rumble of a diesel engine. His skin was leather, tough and aged by decades under the hot beating sun. If his hair wasn't shaved down so short his ears wouldn't have seemed so large, but with a crew cut they looked more like wings. With a stub of an old, long since burned out cigar cemented between his lips, he commanded his men fiercely. He demanded every ounce of energy their bodies could muster, and in return he never asked them to do anything he wouldn't do himself. Simpson respected Sergeant Wilder, but in this moment fear trumped that.

"Yes sir," Simpson replied as he hustled to land on the spot in the dirt where Wilder's finger was now pointing.

"You disobeyed a direct order out there," Wilder roared, leaning his face so close to Simpson's the cigar nudged his chin. "You have ten seconds to explain to me why, after you'd been told to stand down, you took it upon yourself to run away from the LZ and put up a flare to draw the enemy's attention."

"Sir, I didn't see any alternative. We had men with critical injuries, and that was the only way to signal the helo to evacuate them. We needed a decoy."

"No shit," Wilder barked. "But we were completely pinned down. There was no way to get that flare up without someone getting killed. We were going to hunker down for the night. Regroup."

"Those men wouldn't have made it through the night, sir," Simpson replied, trying to stare straight ahead and not waiver under the power of Wilder's voice.

"Oh you're a clairvoyant are you? Or a doctor? You know what tomorrow would have brought?" Wilder yanked the cigar from his mouth and pushed his forehead against Simpson's as he raised his voice another few decibels.

"No sir," Simpson replied, knowing that was where he should stop but continuing anyway. "I thought it was my duty to try to save those men, my brothers. I wanted to try."

"The problem with that is, son," Wilder hissed, his lowered voice actually more frightening than his shouting, "you shouldn't have even survived. There were landmines, heavy gunfire, and enemy combatants everywhere. It was a suicide mission."

Simpson clenched his jaw and raised his chin a fraction of an inch, not wanting to react to that accusation.

"So that's it then," Wilder announced, tucking his cigar back between his teeth and backing away. "You know, I've seen brave men in action before. They risk their lives to make sure their brothers get a chance to get out of this hellhole jungle."

"Yes sir," Simpson said, praying that would be the end of their conversation. He'd disobeyed an order, but his plan had worked. The redirection of the flare had drawn the attention of the enemy and given the helo time to evacuate. They'd even had time to toss a ladder down and evacuate Simpson. Lives were saved.

"No, I'm not lumping you in that category. You're in a whole other world than those men. The difference is the look on their faces when it's over. It's a relief, a sheer adrenaline rush when they complete a mission that risked their lives. I saw your face when that rope dropped down next to you from the copter. You were disappointed. You didn't intend to make it out of there. You were hoping you didn't."

"Sir," Simpson started, but he stopped abruptly when Wilder charged forward and grabbed his collar. "You don't want to live? You don't want to go home? Every man in this jungle is dreaming of his girl, of his mama's home-cooking, and you are hoping to rot out here? That's not the kind of man I want under my command."

"Sir," Simpson interjected again, terrified his actions today and the accusation would be enough to be sent home. "It's not like that."

"Then you better tell me what it is like before I get your ass shipped back to the states, which is every man's dream out here but yours, apparently. You got a ring on your finger; you think your wife deserves to be a widow?"

"She'd be better off, sir." Simpson wished he could take the words back as soon as he'd said them. There was no going back once he'd let the truth escape.

"Hmm," Wilder grunted, seeming to get a clearer picture. "You a drinker? A cheat? You slap her around?"

"No sir," Simpson insisted, breaking his blank stare out into the jungle and turning his gaze to meet Wilder's head on. "I've never done anything like that, never would. I love my wife."

"Then you don't have a damn clue what it means to make her a widow. I have stood at the grave of dozens of men and hugged their young wives. Those women are never the same. Never."

Simpson took the helmet off his head and flipped it over. "This place is hell," he admitted. "But I've seen hell before. People here want me dead, but that's nothing new for me." Pulling out the picture he'd slid into the strap of his helmet, he continued, "You hear it don't you? The men here, how they treat the black soldiers, how they talk about what's going on back home? So much hate in their voices. That's bad enough for my wife," he explained, turning the photo so Wilder could see it. "But to have to be married to me, to have to sacrifice a normal life is too much. I wanted to make sure she had what she needed. My military benefits, our house, but outside of that I don't want her to have to suffer through life with me. It's better if I don't make it home, and if I can save some men that's just gravy."

Wilder snatched the picture from Simpson's hand and began chuckling. It was low at first, almost lost in the noises of the jungle. Then it grew to a full-on hardy laugh that couldn't be contained. It was like an insane person laughing at the voices in his head. Simpson had no clue what had spurred it, but he hoped it would stop.

"You fool," Wilder accused. "You love this girl enough to die out here in this hell? If she loves you even a fraction as much as you love her then you're a damn idiot to toss it away. Come with me." He waved Simpson to follow him into his tent and take a seat on the wooden box of ammunition in the corner. The tent reeked of sweat and cigars, but Simpson was glad to be out of the sun. "What's her name?" Wilder asked.

"Alma," Simpson answered, looking uneasy and desperately wanting the photograph back. "We've known each other since we were children."

Wilder crouched and dug through a bag at his feet. "This here is Gloria," he announced as he flipped a photo of a Native American woman toward Simpson to see. "We've been married for seventeen years. Well sort of. You see it wasn't legal for us to marry back when I first asked her. I spent a month in jail for sharing a house with her. We moved to four states just to try to have a life together. Finally I enlisted, hoping I could give her something better."

"I didn't know," Simpson apologized, feeling stupid for accusing every military meathead of being racist and small-minded.

"I don't go around shoving it in everyone's face because half these guys still have it in their head that it should be illegal. That we should all live separate and not mix races. But I'll tell you one thing, I've never once thought about leaving her for her own good. That's the stupidest piece of crap I've ever heard in my life. You think she's just going to go on and find some other love? Gloria and I have struggled our way through life for a long time, but we've done it together. I wouldn't trade that for any easy kind of love, and she wouldn't either."

Simpson wondered for a moment if he'd actually been killed out there in the jungle today because the idea of a heart to heart with a man like Wilder was too surreal. It had to be a dream. "I want her life to be easy."

"Being a widow, being alone? That's not an easy life, and if she loves you like you say she does then she won't just pick up and get over you. Losing you would break her more than dealing with a little hate out in the world ever could. You smoke?" Wilder offered a cigarette to Simpson who took it happily. The commander yanked a box of matches from his pocket and lit it for him.

Taking in a long burning drag, Simpson felt the reality around him slipping away. He'd convinced himself of one thing for so long; the idea of changing it now rattled him. "I'll probably get blown to bits now that I don't want to anymore," Simpson joked, but Wilder kept a stone face.

"We're moving out of here tonight. In two months we'll all be home in our own beds, and this place will be a distant memory. And whatever war you've got to fight back home is worth it." Wilder tossed his cigar down and grabbed a fresh one, lighting it as he pulled in a few deep breaths.

"I don't know. She deserves the best, and I don't know what kind of life we'll have." Simpson blew a puff of smoke through his lips and watched it as it swirled away.

"None of us know, you moron," Wilder shot back. "But we are all obligated to wait and find out. No bailing early."

"That man changed the course of my entire life," Simpson explained as he watched the fireflies twinkle their way across the front yard of Betty's house.

"That one talk changed your mind?" Piper asked, skepticism an ever-present part of her that Simpson was starting to pick up on.

"No, it took a lot more conversation and some heavy convincing, but eventually I knew he was right. That's not even the extent of how he changed our lives though. When it was over, when we were all home and I was back at the base being debriefed, I got new orders. I was to move my family and myself to a new post. An island somewhere out in the Pacific Ocean I'd sure as hell never heard of. It was far off the coast of Hawaii and the only instruction I was given was to report to duty in a week with my wife to be relocated for a classified mission. It took a mountain of paperwork and lots of pulled strings but we were able to have Nate come with us. It's normally impossible to finagle something like that but looking back I'd imagine Wilder had a lot to do with it. I couldn't believe Alma was willing to just sell the house we'd bought and come on this insane adventure with me."

"What were you sent there to do?" Frankie asked as she

munched another handful of popcorn and looked inquisitively at him.

"Two weeks after we arrived I still had no idea. All I knew was the island was a tropical paradise, and we were waiting for other men and their families to come and join us. The house was this perfect cottage, and I didn't care what they ask us to do, I wanted to stay on that island forever. It was so quiet, practically deserted, and I'd never seen Alma so relaxed and joyful."

"I can't imagine what kind of mission you'd have to do there. Was it training?" Michael asked, looking completely intrigued.

"Apparently Wilder had been asked to lead a group of men in a study regarding race in the military and its impact on such things as morale, success rates of missions, and overall impact on the military experience. Most people assumed it was a cakewalk objective given to a man who'd risked his life and won countless battles over a long career. And they'd assumed right. While we were tasked with collecting data, opinions, and reviewing particular battles and firefights that occurred over the years, for the most part this mission was a gift given to Wilder and he was kind enough to pass it on to others. Every family who arrived on the island to work under him was part of an interracial marriage, or the product of one. He created this place where there were so many different colors and ethnicities and backgrounds there was no real majority, no one group to be biased against. It gave Alma and me the chance to experience a real marriage without fear or sacrifice. It gave us a chance to be husband and wife."

"That's incredible," Clay exclaimed as he walked across the porch and refilled glasses with wine or juice. "How long did it last?"

"Only a few years, that's all the military had sanctioned the project for, but Wilder was well-liked by so many that when one post would finish he'd make sure all of us ended up at another friendly post where we could be close to our families and live without so much bias. I mean, you couldn't avoid it all together, but he'd find posts that would limit it. Over the years his wife, Gloria, and Alma became great friends. Like I said, he changed the course of our lives. I don't know what we'd have done without that."

"But the distance, the remoteness of your locations was hard," Betty admitted. "There would have been times I'd have liked to go see you, to be close, and it always felt impossible."

"The distance is what gave us the freedom we were looking for. Our boys were not exposed to anything we had to go through. They had time to just be kids. When Wilder died we'd both already retired from the military and had actually been living away from each other for almost a decade, but I still felt like I'd lost my father. That's really what he'd become to me. He did more for me than my father ever did."

With a monstrous yawn, Frankie rubbed at her eyes and then immediately regretted it. "I'm not tired," she defended preemptively. "I know you're gonna say we should go home now."

"The story's done for tonight, kiddo," Simpson announced as he slapped his hands down on his thighs and then stood. "Plus your questions are dwindling down. Don't want to waste them all tonight."

"Forty-nine," Frankie counted, looking down to her notebook at some hash marks. "You promised you'd answer them all. Don't you dare forget it."

"If I forgot for even a second, I'm betting you'd be there to remind me. No getting anything past you, I can see that now."

"She's persistent," Betty chimed in as she pinched Frankie's cheek affectionately. "It's in her genes."

CHAPTER 13

Most of his life Simpson had dreamed of days where he had nothing to do. Just lie back, twiddle his thumbs, and watch the hours tick by. That's what he thought a perfectly calm day would be like. Now that he'd been living that life for weeks in Edenville he realized how badly he missed being busy. Being tired. Being needed. As imposed upon as he felt by the weekly dinners at Betty's when he'd arrived, now it seemed like they didn't come frequently enough. On days when the school bus would stop at the end of the driveway, dropping off the precious cargo that was Frankie, he felt relieved. He wasn't sure if she'd be by today; the bus wouldn't be coming for another fifteen minutes, if it came at all. So he was determined to cast off his idle hands and make himself useful.

The shed outside Betty's house was cluttered and dark, but Simpson managed to find what he was looking for. The squeaks in the porch swing and screen door could be easily remedied with some oil. It wasn't much in the way of helping out, but it was a start. He'd begun taking notice of small things around the house he could repair. Pointing the flashlight around the lopsided shed one more time, he took stock of what other tools might aid him on future projects. The jumbled beat of tires rolling over the gravel in the dirt driveway piqued his curiosity. Betty was up at the house finishing a new recipe she was testing for the menu, and Clay was holding down the fort at the restaurant until around six. No one else had mentioned coming by today that he could recall, so it was enough to make him hesitate at the slanted door of the old shed and watch the car pull hastily toward the front of the house.

It was a nondescript red sedan and, though he couldn't pinpoint why, he took note of the license plate number, quickly committing it to memory. A pang in his gut gnawed at him. Betty's door was certainly always open to friends, but something about this felt off.

He watched as Betty stepped determinedly out the screen door, the telltale squeak he was trying to fix ringing out, followed by a quick thud as it closed behind her. It was her body language that sealed the deal for Simpson. Rarely were her arms ever folded across her chest like they were now. One eyebrow was cocked high above the other, and her lips were pressed together tightly.

The car door of the sedan swung open so forcefully it seemed as though it might come straight off its hinges. Out tumbled a round man with rosy cheeks, who, if not for the expression of anger on his face and the lack of a white beard, could have been mistaken for Santa Claus.

"Norm, what's the problem now? My grass too high? My leaves blowing into the street again?" Betty called from the porch toward the man who tripped and stumbled his way to the stair railing.

"You wish it were something that small," Norm hissed back, grabbing at the railing to steady himself. "We have ourselves a much bigger problem. But the good news is you can fix it 'fore anything bad happens to you or yours."

With that threat, Simpson felt his hands clench into fists, and

DANIELLE STEWART

he stepped one foot out of the shed. With a subtle wave of her hand Betty halted him. Unsure if it was part of her plan or for his own protection he stopped, but remained completely ready to react if needed.

"Norm, if you've got something to say just be out with it. I don't have all day to listen to you ramble on about me and mine." Betty perched her hands on her hips and stared down at Norm, looking thoroughly annoyed. Her irritation seemed to fuel his.

"Betty, you think you're better than everyone else, don't you?" Norm growled, slamming his hand down on the railing of the stairs.

"Not everyone," Betty hummed. "Maybe just better than people who come around here looking for fights where there doesn't need to be any."

"There does," Norm insisted. "I was just down at Calhoon's for happy hour and heard your son-in-law bought up that plot of land where the old school used to be. He intends to start some kind of memorial. That ain't gonna happen."

"It's private property now, much like this is, I'll remind you. That means you don't get any say on what happens here. I'm not even entirely sure why you'd be so vehemently opposed to a memorial." Betty kept her chin high as she looked down at Norm appraisingly.

"You know damn well my daddy was there that night. So was yours. Don't you have any loyalty to your parents? Of course you don't; I already know that. My daddy used to tell me all the time how you pretty much spit in the face of your parents, like an ungrateful heathen." Norm took one step toward Betty, and that was close enough for Simpson's liking.

"Looks like you have company," Simpson called loudly in a deep voice as he crossed the grass back toward the house.

"Ah," Norm groaned. "Here's another one. Your riffraff

shelter for the wayward has another guest I nearly forgot about. What's this one, a psychopath? A thief?"

"Just your run of the mill house guest," Simpson explained as he nudged his way past Norm to stand by Betty's side. "You can call me S. I'm a friend of Clay's. Don't think I know your name," Simpson said, looking Norm over and knowing exactly who he was. He was the spitting image of his father, and just seeing the man brought back rage.

"You don't need to know my name," Norm slurred back. "All you need to know is why I'm here. That's to stop Betty from kicking a hornet's nest. She has no idea what I'm capable of." Norm took another step forward.

"Well if you won't tell me your name, I'll have to come up with something to call you. How about I just call you bourbon, since there seems to be a cloud of it around you," Simpson joked, stepping an inch in front of Betty.

"You wanna dance, Yankee?" Norm asked, balling his hands into fists and raising them up in front of his face.

"You're not really what I like in a dance partner," Simpson jested, inciting the man's anger even further.

"Oh that's right," Norm chuckled. "I'm much more that teacher Ray's type than yours."

"I doubt it," Simpson retorted with a wry smile. "The man's gay; he's not blind."

"You son of a bitch," Norm shouted as he stumbled up the last two stairs, tripping and planting his face into Simpson's chest. He righted himself and stumbled backward. "If you don't get that son-in-law of yours to change his plans, I will bring hellfire down on all of you. Every degenerate and murderer you've let through these doors in the last ten years—I will unearth every secret they have. I know things about the trouble that girl Piper got in. I've got friends on the police force who know secrets about what she's done, about the murder in the cabin all those year ago. If you are so damn set on digging up and distorting my father's legacy, you can know damn well I'll be right there taking down every single person you've ever given refuge to here."

Simpson scoffed, but from the corner of his eye he could see Betty was rattled. Clearly Piper wasn't a murderer, but if he based it just on Betty's reaction to the threat, he might have some doubts.

"In what way would I be defaming your father's legacy? The man was Klan, he committed crimes, he hated, and he hurt people. I never spat in my parents' faces, not literally or figuratively; best I can remember they were the ones spitting on people. You were a toddler at the time, you have no way of knowing what they really did, what they were capable of, but I lived it. And it was terrifying. But I'll tell you one thing I'm not scared of, and that's the truth. Can you say the same?"

"I'll bring out the truth, Betty," Norm assured, waving a finger in her direction. "I'll bring out the truth on every single one of these people you've given refuge to. Including you," Norm laughed, pointing now at Simpson. "I don't know what your story is, but Lord knows you must have one or else Betty wouldn't have you here. You haven't set foot in town, so she's hiding you, I'm sure. Now, I'll give Michael until tomorrow evening to change his plans before I start calling in an army of people to destroy what you hold dear."

"It's been my experience, Norm," Betty said coolly, "that making threats against this family doesn't tend to end well for the person doing it. I'm sorry your daddy didn't leave a better legacy. Hell, I'm sorry mine didn't. But that doesn't change the fact that people died. They were murdered and burned and then forced to be forgotten by a town frozen by fear. You want to try to bully me out of honoring them, then I'll put you down in the same category as the Klan, and I'll treat you the same damn way I treated them. People in this town aren't going to stand for your nonsense. They had every right to step in where school was concerned; I can respect that. But now we're talking private property and a cause they can support. You won't get them on your side, not the majority of them."

"I won't be looking here in town for support," Norm sneered. "Most people with any loyalty to our fathers and their cause have moved on, but I bet they'd be happy to move right back in if it meant stopping you from twisting history into whatever you want. There was anger on both sides of that argument, that night and for decades leading up to it. Don't paint our fathers as villains and these dead people as martyrs. They were violent, they needed to be stopped, and my daddy put his life on the line to keep this town safe. To keep it the way it was always meant to be. If you put that memorial up, you'll be telling this town that wasn't the case."

"Then I'd be telling them the truth," Betty replied flatly.

The familiar rumbling engine of a school bus echoed its way up the road. Simpson knew if the bus was stopping, Frankie would be getting out, and that upped the ante on this situation significantly for him. He'd known Betty to be a woman who could, and often did, fend for herself. Bringing a child, especially a strong-willed and opinioned child, into an argument with a sloppy drunk bigot was dangerous.

"You," Norm shouted, flipping his shirt up from his hip and putting a hand on the butt of a holstered gun. Simpson saw red and a long forgotten gut reaction took over. His elbow flew to Norm's neck as his other hand yanked the gun from the holster. With a fluid twist of his body he brought the gun up and used it to strike the back of Norm's head sending him toppling over, thudding against the wood floor of the porch.

"My, my, Simpson, the Army did right by you," Betty observed with wide eyes.

"Better give Bobby a call," Simpson said, quickly dropping

the clip out of the gun and popping the one in the chamber out. He placed the disassembled gun down on the small table by the rocking chairs and then sat. "I'm worried we just started a war."

"We did," Betty admitted, touching Simpson's shoulder gently. "But don't worry, we've got some skilled soldiers on our side."

"Don't think I can get him up and off this porch by the time Frankie comes up that driveway," Simpson apologized.

"It'll do her good to see what happens to people with no good sense in their head and too much bourbon in their belly. We'll call it a life lesson."

CHAPTER 14

"Wait, what exactly did you do with him?" Piper asked Bobby nervously as she skillfully tied her daughter's hair into pigtails.

"Simpson and I loaded him into my squad car, and before he came to I dropped him back off in front of Calhoon's," Bobby explained with a shrug.

"Where in the world did my husband go?" Piper asked jokingly. "This is the man who used to incessantly beat the drum of right and wrong, and now you're dumping people off after they get assaulted?"

"Trust me," Simpson explained, "that man had it coming. He was about to pull a gun. I've lived outside the South too long. I forgot how many people have a license to carry and how that license doesn't go away just because they're drunk."

"What do you think he did when he woke up?" Piper asked, clearly looking rattled by the events. "He said he was going to unearth all our secrets. I'm guessing hitting him in the head just fueled the fire." She patted her daughter gently on the backside and gestured for her to scoot inside the house.

"Sounded like the blustering of a man emboldened by booze, if you ask me." Simpson was trying to act casual, but in reality he was shaken by the encounter. "What's he really got on any of you? He won't find out anything on me; I've been living as a different person for decades. If the military never caught onto it, then he's not going to dig it up."

"We've got secrets," Piper whispered, looking back between Bobby and Betty. "Ones that would certainly ruin our lives if they were exposed. We warned you that you weren't the only one who could stir up drama. Our share of it has been pretty extensive over the last ten years."

Anxiety coursed through Simpson's veins. This was exactly what he was afraid would happen coming back here. Well, all right, not exactly this, but he knew his presence back in this town would cause ripples that could possibly turn to tidal waves. "Then you have to make Michael abandon his plans. That's a good plot of land; I'm sure he can recoup his money if he sold it. If you've really all got something to lose, it's not worth it."

"You'll be hard-pressed to convince Frankie of that," Bobby chuckled. "She's practically got the plans for the place drafted. Plus Michael reached out to the daughters of Ellie Perry, who was murdered that day. They're coming out here in a few days to talk. It's already in motion."

"Then put the brakes on," Simpson said sharply. "It's not worth crossing this man or having him involve other people who had some sort of loyalty to the Klan back then. You can't go up against them."

"You say that," Piper interjected, "because you don't know what we've been up against before. I sat here and listened to Betty tell us what happened that night, and I believed her. And if that is the case then those three people who were murdered deserve to be remembered. The secrets Norm is talking about, I'll admit, are most likely mine, and I'm willing to take that risk and fight to make sure this still happens. I mean, who could he really call in from other places that still feel like the Klan was in the right, that they were heroes? In this day and age, who would really believe that?"

"The Sons of Allegiance is who," Bobby interjected solemnly. "It's a group of people who believe exactly as Norm does. They don't go so far as to associate themselves with present day hate groups, but their goal is to preserve the righteousness they feel the previous generation was living by. They don't push a message to promote segregation, extremism, or hate of any kind. They just try to humanize the Klan and say there is another side to the story other than the one history tells."

"You think Norm is a part of this Sons of Allegiance?" Betty asked dismissively, waving off the idea that a man like Norm could really and truly believe there was another side of that story to be told.

"Probably not officially anyway," Bobby explained. "But I'm betting that's what he meant when he said he'd be calling people in. They, or someone like them, could surely show up."

"What exactly do these people do? They still burning crosses and holding late night meetings in the dark?" Simpson felt his blood boil at the idea that hate still existed in the world.

"No, nothing like that. They hand out flyers, and they petition. They stall construction, and they lobby to block what they don't agree with. As you can imagine, it's wildly unsuccessful considering the view the majority of the world has on civil rights and how history judges that time. But they're usually a nuisance nonetheless. My biggest concern would be more about Norm's threats to come after anyone you've had living in this house. I'm not fool enough to think this town has never caught wind of some of the unorthodox ways we've accomplished things. For the most part I'm guessing everyone has overlooked it, since in the end we tend to get what's best, but if someone dug deep enough, on any of us, there might be trouble. Maybe Simpson's right; maybe we need to back off."

"Because some drunk fool got mouthy? If people had backed off that easy back then, we'd still be fighting for the right for everyone to eat where they like. This stuff isn't supposed to be easy." Betty moved her hands animatedly as she made her point.

"You aren't talking about the memorial, are you?" Frankie asked, pressing her tiny face against the screen door.

"You're supposed to be doing your math homework," Betty scolded, and then softened her face. "This is just an obstacle, darling, one I'm sure we grown-ups can handle. That's your daddy pulling in, and I promised him you'd be done with your work by the time he got here. Don't make a liar out of me."

Frankie nodded, turned on her heels, and headed into the living room. Michael skidded his car to a stop and jumped out in a flash, angrily slamming his door behind him.

"That son a bitch pulled a gun around my daughter?" he yelled, stomping his feet up the porch.

Simpson tried to calm him, though he knew it wasn't likely. "She wasn't even off the bus yet, and technically I knocked him out before he could pull it. For all we know he was just scratching his stomach, and I overreacted."

"Good, when my kid's around, be sure to overreact." Michael nodded his silent gratitude at Simpson and paced around the porch. "What the hell is his problem? Why would Norm care this much?"

"His daddy told him a very different version of not only that night, but what the Klan was all about. He feels that creating a memorial undermines the truth the way he sees it."

"The truth the way he sees it is not the truth," Michael countered dismissively.

"Well, tell that to the newspaper articles written in that era. Tell that to the groups apparently dedicated to defending the honor and memory of the Klan. He's not alone in this, and, just like most people, he believes what he heard over and over again growing up. Or at least he wants to believe it."

Michael stopped pacing and looked over at Piper. "It's not like we're all squeaky clean here. We don't need any extra attention on our mistakes or our pasts."

"Are you suggesting we just give up?" Betty asked with a threatening eyebrow raised at him. "It'd be the first time I've heard you propose that."

"We've got quite a bit on the line here. We're not kids anymore running around Edenville trying to solve crimes and find justice. We're parents; we're responsible for more than just ourselves. We have our kids to think about," Michael whispered, peering through the screen door to ensure Frankie wasn't listening.

"Exactly," Betty replied, countering his point with the same argument. "You've got your kids to think about. It sounds like even more reason to make sure they see us fighting for what's right."

"I don't disagree," Simpson sighed. "I'm just wondering if we have the right fight. If now is the right time. Aren't there other ways to make the same point without causing any trouble? Maybe it's better for us to just keep quiet for a bit."

"That sounds an awful lot like what you and I had to do most our childhood, Simpson," Betty cut back. "I swore I would make sure my kids and grandkids had it different. I'm not going in that house and telling Frankie it's too hard to do what she thinks is right, so she should stop. That we're all stopping."

Michael let out an exhausted grunt and flopped into the porch swing. "I guess we've got ourselves another battle."

CHAPTER 15

"Marline and April, I can't thank you enough for coming," Betty announced as she crossed the floor of the restaurant and greeted the two women who had just come in. "You both have your mother's smile."

"We must," April retorted flatly. "Our father didn't have a smile. Or if he did he kept it to himself." The buzzing energy of excitement evaporated, and the large group that was Betty's family fell awkwardly silent.

"I remember he was a tough man," Betty agreed. "But he did have a passion for silly knock-knock jokes."

The two girls looked at each other in disbelief. "Perhaps we're not talking about the same man then. I never heard my father tell a joke a day in his life. The man just worked and frowned," Marline explained.

"How was the trip into town?" Michael asked, breaking the tension that was growing. "I'm guessing neither of you have been to Edenville before."

"No, our father forbade it. We've never even been to our mother's grave. Now that we're here, come to find out I don't think there's a grave. Edenville was a real sore spot; he couldn't really ever bring himself to talk about her or what happened. Anything Marline and I found out was from research we did on our own. That's why we were shocked to get your call. We didn't think many people still cared much about what happened."

"And to be frank," Marline said, "I didn't expect it to be so many white people."

"We do care," Betty was quick to shoot back. "I was there the night your mother was killed. I knew her, though she never taught my grade. She was very kind and meek, soft spoken in the warmest way."

"Why did you ask us here?" April questioned, seeming more tense by the minute. "You'll excuse us for being curt, but while our father had little to say about what happened in Edenville, he had plenty to say about how much he hated it. He didn't paint this place as very welcoming."

"I can understand that," Betty admitted. Simpson watched the scene and had to continually remind himself to breathe. April, the eldest daughter, was a dead ringer for her mother, and the sight of her made his knees weak. It had been agreed that Simpson wouldn't tell the girls he had been there that night or who he really was. The secret was still as important as ever. "We asked you here because we intend to make a memorial to honor those who died that night at the school. It's long overdue, but we've begun the process of bringing attention to what happened, and we wanted to talk to you about it. As the children of one of the victims, we wanted to involve you. If that's something you'd like, of course."

"You're saying Edenville is different? They're sorry for what happened and for the death of my mother? People here are finally ready to admit they were wrong? Because when April and I started researching our mother's death we found a lot of stonewalling and clearly fabricated information. I don't think for a moment our mother set her own car on fire in an act of protest

121

and then provoked the Klan with threats of violence." Marline's face was stoic as she spoke.

"You shouldn't believe that, because it's not true. There was no provocation at all. It was an attack, and a planned one at that," Simpson said and then quickly busied himself by wiping down a few tables that were already clean.

"You were there too?" April asked, eyeing him closely.

"No," he answered quickly, a jumpy nervousness taking over his body. "Betty told us all what happened. There's no doubt in my mind."

"Well, we want to know the details. We want to understand what the last moments of our mother's life were like. It's important to us. That night didn't just take our mama from us; it took the best parts of our daddy, too." April reached a hand out and touched her sister on the shoulder, both clearly shaken by the idea of actually hearing the truth.

"Our father gave up," Marline stuttered out. "He didn't even fight to get justice for our mother. Our whole lives we've wanted to know more. We've always wanted to understand better, but he just couldn't bring himself to talk about it. I just wished he'd loved us enough to try."

Michael cleared his throat and stepped forward. "A couple days after your mother was killed your father was arrested for speeding. I spoke to Betty to see if she had any memory of this since the police report was very vague. She told me your father never drove."

"That's right," April said perking up with curiosity. "He had a glass eye and the vision in his other eye wasn't great. He was never able to get his license."

"Right," Michael said, nodding his head. "Betty informed me it was well-known the speeding charge was bogus. When he was detained he was threatened and told if he didn't leave town and stop causing a scene he'd be tossed in jail and buried in the system while his two daughters were sent to a home for abandoned children. I believe that's why he didn't fight harder for justice. I believe that's why none of the families involved fought for some type of conviction. They were likely all threatened and chased out of town."

Marline and April looked at each other with wet eyes and crumpled chins, trying to hold their composure. Before anyone could speak, the bell over the door chimed.

"We're closed," Betty sang, spinning around. Seeing the unwanted guest she added curtly, "Didn't you see the sign?"

"Awful lot of people in here for being closed," Norm pointed out as he eyed the group. His hand sat high on his hip just above his holstered gun.

Bobby sidestepped Piper and put himself just inches from Norm. "The restaurant is closed. Leave or I will arrest you."

"I was just coming to give Betty an update. I'd heard a couple of girls had rolled into town. Daughters of one of the protestors at the school is the rumor." Norm lifted up to his tiptoes to peer over Bobby's shoulder.

"There was no protest there that day," Betty shot back. "There were just innocent teachers and students trying to attend a school dance."

"So you've filled their heads with lies already. How convenient." Norm threw his hands up quickly as Bobby inched forward, aggressively grabbing his shoulder. "I'm going. I just wanted Betty to know she isn't the only one with people coming to town. I've got some folks with vested interest who want their story to be told, I'm sure. One of which is a relation of yours."

"Excuse me?" Jules asked, waving Bobby to stand down for a second.

"The Grafton boy who is still living, your late husband's brother, is coming to town. He'll be here to see you *try* to break ground at your new property." Norm puffed out his chest as though he'd just called checkmate.

Simpson felt his already weak knees give way, and the chair he tried to brace himself on tumbled over.

"Get him out of here, Bobby, before I toss him on his ass," Michael shouted, spinning quickly to try to aid Simpson.

"I'm going," Norm said, yanking the door open and whistling condescendingly as he stepped out into the darkness of the night.

When Simpson was back on his feet, Michael moved him over toward a booth to sit. Quick as a whip Piper was in front of him with a glass of cold water. "I'm fine," Simpson insisted, trying to drive all the eyes on him away.

"So I was right," April said, peering out the window toward the street. "Edenville hasn't changed. Not everyone is looking forward to a memorial. There will be trouble."

Betty looked over at the girls with an empathetic gaze. "We'd all understand if you don't want any part of this. It was our intention to let you know our plans and give you the opportunity to take part in it whichever way you wanted. I'm sorry to say, yes, there will likely be some difficulty and maybe even some obstacles. You girls don't need to face that, not after everything you've lost in Edenville already."

Marline looked over at her sister and grinned, drawing curious looks. "The reason we asked the question wasn't because we were afraid to face any opposition here in Edenville. It's because we wanted the chance to do what our father didn't. Now that I know someone doesn't want this memorial, I'm going to do everything in my power to make sure it happens. You tell us what you need. Money, resources, man power. April and I will find a way to get it."

"My kind of girls," Betty laughed as she opened her arms and pulled them in for a hug.

"We have a multifaceted plan in place right now," Michael

explained as he pulled a file from his briefcase. "On the actual property we hope to create a park and garden with a plaque commemorating the date and those killed. I've had some rough plans drawn up by a contractor friend of mine. We're breaking ground on Saturday. I've also petitioned Congress to pass a non-binding resolution to honor the people who died at the school. I've got a few contacts up on the hill who might be able to help, but it'll be slow going. The mayor of Edenville also seems open to some ideas that could involve the town more directly, but I'm still working on that front. In my experience, Edenville is split up the middle on these issues. Some feel like the future is where we should pour our energy while others feel, until those skeletons are pulled out into the open, there is no way to move forward. Some might come around, others might cause trouble, but there is hope."

"And?" Marline asked, shaking her head and sending her beaded earrings clanking in either direction. "You didn't mention anything about the status of the murder case. You're a lawyer right? Where are you in getting it reopened? He's a cop; he must be able to put some pressure on at least the local authorities, and then perhaps we can create some congressional pressure to get the case reopened." She pointed over at Bobby expectantly.

"It was never a federal case," Michael replied. "We wouldn't technically need any other entity to step in and order the case reopened, but that's not on our radar. After giving it a lot of thought, we feel like dredging up the past wouldn't serve the purpose we're hoping for. The people in question, those in power in the Klan on the day of the attack, are either dead or old and infirm. We aren't looking to put a black mark on Edenville, just looking to celebrate the people we lost."

"Because you just hugged me so warmly I'm going to refrain from cursing," Marline said, drawing in a deep centering breath. "I don't care if these people are catatonic or gasping their last breaths, I want the people involved in the murder of our mother brought to justice. I am a lawyer in D.C. and have absolutely no intention of letting this miscarriage of justice go on another moment. My entire life I respected our father's wishes to let sleeping dogs lie, but I also worked to make sure when the time came I could honor our mother properly. April has endless contacts in D.C. after running successful congressional campaigns. You give us the information on the petition you've filed for the non-binding resolution, and she'll push it through. We appreciate your valiant attempts to pay tribute to those lost, but we're looking for something more. We want justice."

Piper gently stepped toward them both and softened her face with a smile. "I've been where you are. It can be overwhelming to try to chase down the people who've wronged you. It's very easy to lose sight of the bigger picture. You may feel angry and obviously what happened was an atrocity, but don't you think reopening the case will be more volatile and offer disappointing results, considering the status of most if not all of the defendants? Doesn't memorializing the victims, bringing attention to what happened, seem like a better use of your energy?"

"No," April replied flatly. "There is ample precedent for this. In Mississippi there have been six trials for forty-year-old cold cases. Two of which ended with prosecutions and jail time for the defendants. We want that."

"Regardless of the collateral damage and opposition?" Betty asked, her voice thick with concern. "People here are willing to pay homage to those who died, but what you're talking about is something very different. It shines a light in many an eye."

Marline nodded her head vehemently. "Good. If there are people here who were involved, I hope the light blinds them. Let them come counter the search for justice and see how they fare."

"It's not only those who were personally involved you'll stir up," Simpson interjected. "That time in Edenville is something many want to forget, not just because bad people did bad things, but because good people did nothing to stop them. The guilt, the burden of that on them and their children and grandchildren, is perhaps a wider net than you had in mind."

"Better to catch many in it than no one," Marline reasoned, grabbing her bag off the table in front of her and slinging it over her shoulder. "April and I are on your side. We want to help with the plans you've created. We're grateful for them. But we aren't going to stop there, and if it means people here want a fight, we're prepared to bring them one. I'm sure our mother lived many of her days in fear. My sister and I aren't afraid."

"We're grateful for any help you can provide," Michael said with a smile as he shook their hands on their way to the door. "Do you have a place to stay here in town?"

"We're not staying in town," Marline replied. "The better hotels were just over the line in Monroe so we found rooms there. Maybe some distance will do us good if people are as angry as you're worried they might be. We'll be at the groundbreaking ceremony on Saturday, and I'm sure you'll be seeing us around town as we start the initial process to try to get the case reopened. I hope we can count on you all."

CHAPTER 16

"What the hell are we going to do now?" Simpson asked, rubbing at his temples where tension had started to gather.

"We can figure this out," Michael announced, sounding more like he was trying to convince himself. "The case may not even get reopened."

"If they request the case to be opened, it will be. My precinct is hungry for cold cases because of the attention they garner. If the children of one of the victims show interest, they'll move forward. We should prepare for that."

"How?" Simpson asked frantically as he slid out of the booth and gripped the wall to steady himself. "This was in our worst-case-scenario bucket. If the case is reopened they'll realize my body was never found at the scene. Someone will put it together. I can't stay here."

"Easy," Piper said, clutching his arm. "We can still get out ahead of this. There has to be more we can do."

Every eye turned expectantly toward Michael for an answer. "I'm not sure what our options are at this point. His brother is coming to town. It would be highly unlikely he wouldn't recognize you. If people are looking for a way to throw a wrench in either the case or the memorial, we'll be giving them the ammunition to do it. Maybe you should go."

"No," Betty insisted, slicing her hand through the air definitively. "He can stay at the house. No one even needs to see him. If the case gets reopened, we can come up with some explanation for why the body wasn't found. It was a chaotic scene that was surely compromised in all the commotion."

"Betty," Clay spoke gently, slipping his hand into hers, "if this becomes an investigation and you're questioned, anything you said could be making a false statement. If it ever went to trial you could go as far as committing perjury. We have to think this through."

"Whether he's here or not, that would happen," Betty defended. "I know him to be alive, and if I don't disclose that, and trust me I will not, I'll be committing a crime."

"Everyone take a breath," Bobby insisted. "Maybe we can talk to April and Marline and explain the situation. There's a chance they'd understand and decide not to pursue opening the case."

"I won't ask them to do that," Simpson insisted, shrugging Piper off his arm. "Why the hell shouldn't they have justice? If not for my involvement in all this, can you honestly say you wouldn't be pursuing the same thing? You all seem to be fairly persistent. I'm guessing you'd be running around trying to solve this case on your own. You'd be making sure those involved pay for their crimes. If not for me, this would all be different."

No one had an answer to that painful truth. He'd spent enough time with each of them now to know he was holding all this back. It was the position he'd put them in that kept them from doing what they all felt was right. He knew there was only one way to make this problem disappear. The corners of the web he'd woven over the years needed to be snipped.

"Guess what?" Betty sighed. "Nothing can be fixed tonight.

I've got some food in the kitchen for all of us. What time is Mrs. Withers dropping off the kids?"

"She'll be by with them in about an hour," Piper said, looking down at her watch. "But she was going to feed them dinner first."

"Then we eat now and worry later," Betty decided, heading for the kitchen with Clay at her heels.

Not long after, trays and trays of food came out, including the pineapple dessert that transported Simpson back to Winnie's kitchen. It was a strange magic that tore at his insides. Is this what Alma wanted when she sent him back here? Would she understand why he couldn't do it anymore?

"We're going to clean up. You guys head out now that the kids are back," Betty suggested as she shooed them all toward the door.

"We'll give you a lift home, Simpson," Michael offered as he held the door open for his family.

"I might go for a walk," Simpson said, absentmindedly staring at the stars and remembering his days of using them to understand his location in the world.

"Is that a good idea?" Piper asked, looking over at Bobby to intervene but he just shrugged in that *he's a grown-up and can do what he wants* kind of way.

"I'll go with you if you don't mind." Michael kissed Jules and squeezed Frankie. "Bobby, can you get them home safely for me? I'll give Simpson a lift after our walk and be home soon."

"Of course." Bobby slapped his friend's back and rounded up his family.

Piper smiled and nudged Bobby. "I told you that minivan was the right choice. I'm sure you hardly miss that old pickup at all."

Michael and Simpson began their stroll toward Main Street with a chuckle. "The things we do for the women we love," Michael jested.

"I'm living proof of that," Simpson retorted. "I'd be drunk as a skunk in a hammock and sporting a sunburn right now if not for Alma."

"You still convinced that would have been better?" Michael asked, pretending to look interested in the windows of the quiet shops they passed.

"No," Simpson replied, shaking his head. "I'm ready to say Alma was right. It's helped me to come here. I'm glad to know people care about the things that happened and are willing to fight for them. It makes me happy to see things have changed enough to know a kid like yours can do well instead of being persecuted. But I can't see a point in my staying past this. If there's a war coming there is no point in giving the other side ammunition. The idea of one of my brothers coming back to spread the hate he started all those years ago . . . I just don't think that's what Alma was thinking when she told me to come back here. Maybe I've accomplished everything I was meant to. Perhaps it's diminishing returns from this point on."

"Are you making a case to me?" Michael asked, stuffing his hands in his pockets.

"You're the man to do that, don't you think? They all look to you for your opinion. Even if they don't like it right away, they are more likely to come around if they hear you say my leaving is for the good of everyone."

"You made a promise to Frankie. She's got a list of questions left for you. I'm not sure she's ready for you to leave yet."

"Is she ready to see me go to jail? Is she ready to see her sweet little grandmother arrested for conspiracy and fraud?"

"Come on," Michael laughed, tossing his head back. "There is nothing little and sweet about Betty."

"Michael," Simpson cut in with an air of desperation on his tongue, "you know this is the best thing. Tell me now if there would be a way to get Betty off the hook for this."

"I've been giving that a lot of thought. The only thing that really ties her to this is the letters. Phone calls to Alma couldn't necessarily be linked to her knowing you were alive. She never traveled out to see you over the years. The letters are truly the only proof she knew you were alive."

"Good to know," Simpson said, nodding his head as he thought through every scenario. "You're in pretty good shape; you up for a long walk?"

"Sure," Michael shrugged. "As long as you're not thinking up some big exit strategy. If you steal all Betty's letters and leave town, she'll never forgive you."

"No, nothing like that." They reached the edge of Main Street and stepped off toward the woods. "You've got a flashlight on that fancy phone of yours, right?"

"Yes, but I'll admit I'm getting tired of having to go into the woods with you. Can't we ever just drive?"

"What's the fun in that? This is how I got to Winnie's house for years. I know these woods like the back of my hand."

"That's where we're going?" Michael asked, shooting Simpson a sideways glance. "That's like a few miles isn't it?"

"Oh come on, Marine, don't tell me you can't hike anymore?" Simpson joked, as he pulled some branches back and ducked his way through the thicker section of the woods they were approaching.

"Come on, old man," Michael laughed. "Pick up the pace."

After traipsing their way through woods that had grown significantly thicker over the years, Simpson had to admit he was more exhausted than he thought he would be. As a kid he'd made this trip in a run multiple times per week and had never broken a sweat. As they walked through the edge of the woods they found themselves on the ledge that looked down on what was once rows of shacks. The moon was nearly full, and the light it cast made Michael's phone flashlight unnecessary.

"They're gone," Simpson lamented, a pang of sadness wrenching in his stomach. The ravine had been completely cleared of any sign of what used to exist there. No shacks stood, no fences, and no old water well pipes. All that was left was plowed over earth and clumps of wildflowers. If you didn't know what had existed here before, you might stumble on this ravine and think it beautiful. But if you knew everything that had been destroyed, the void would make this place ugly.

"I'm sure the shacks became uninhabitable at some point, and it was safer to knock them down. I read after the incident at the school there was a mass exodus of people fleeing West Edenville." Michael put his hands on his hips as he worked to catch his breath as well.

"I've just pictured it in my head the exact same way. I thought nothing had changed. I wanted to come back here and see Winnie's house still standing. I don't even know why. It shouldn't matter."

"It matters," Michael insisted. "That's why we're doing what we are doing. It's not acceptable to cover everything over and pretend it never happened. There should be places people can go and reflect on the legacy of Edenville. The good, the bad, the ugly: all of it deserves a place. I know this is getting more complicated. Things look bleak and messy, but I still think we're doing what's right."

"I don't want it to just disappear. I don't want April and Marline to have to keep living with the burden of not knowing what happened to their mother. I know what happened, Michael. I was right there. I was inches from her and watched the light leave her eyes. If they want to know what happened, then who am I to hold onto this truth? Who am I to block them from getting what they need? I feel like everything I did over the years was about self-preservation. This is bigger than me. It always has been."

"I need to know what your plan is, Simpson. Don't sideswipe me with something I can't help you get out from under. Involve me, even if you don't want to tell everyone, tell me."

"There's nothing to tell at this point," Simpson sighed. "I don't have any kind of plan. I don't know what I'll do. I just know whatever I do can't be just for me and my happiness. Alma wanted me to live out my life with some purpose and some peace, and that's not going to come by putting myself first."

"Fine," Michael acquiesced. "Just remember that whatever you do will have an impact on the people here who care for you. Just like with Alma, disappearing *for their own good* isn't fair."

Simpson grunted his agreement as he looked down for another long moment over the field. Closing his eyes he conjured visions of how much life was once here. It wasn't filled with riches or luxuries, but it was overflowing with love in a way he'd never found since.

"Ready to trek back, Marine, or you need to catch your breath?" Simpson asked, slapping Michael jokingly on the back.

"Don't make me race you," Michael goaded, assuming a running position and then giving way to laughter.

"You're a good man, Michael." Seriousness overtook Simpson's face. "I left Betty here and took from her everyone she considered family. For years I wondered if she'd ever be able to be happy, if she'd ever forgive me for bailing on her. When Stan died I realized the curse I'd left on her, pulling away everyone she loved over and over again. Then the letters started coming, talking about you and Piper and the adventures you brought into her life. Her quiet house was full again, and every year it just got more so. No matter what I do, I can't tell you how grateful I am to know she has you. It makes whatever decision I make a little easier. I'll never be able to thank you for that."

"Keep your gratitude," Michael shot back. "Give me time to

figure out something that might help. That's better than a thank you and a goodbye."

"It must be hard for you," Simpson said, looking him over appraisingly. "You don't often have problems that can't be solved. Every now and then, Michael, we all have to lose."

"Every now and then," Michael agreed. "But not today."

CHAPTER 17

Simpson had laid the groundwork for the unavoidable solution he'd settled on. It meant some sneaking around, which he felt sorry about, but he'd convinced himself in the end everyone would understand. At least he hoped so.

The trouble was Betty was a keen woman and her antennas were up. Ever since that night after he returned from his long walk with Michael she'd been giving him long, knowing looks and suspicious glances. He couldn't let that deter him though. His mind was made up.

"There's a car coming up the driveway," Betty hollered from the kitchen into the family room where Simpson sat reading a magazine.

"Anyone you know?" Simpson asked, rounding the corner and peeking through the lace curtains. "It's an out of state plate, Texas I think."

"You best stay out of sight," Betty commanded as she flattened the wrinkles out of her dress and straightened her hair hastily. "Gosh I'm a damn mess from this humidity. No time for unexpected company to be showing up."

"Just be careful," Simpson reminded her. "I'll be right here on the other side of this window, listening, if you have any trouble. Who knows what kind of riffraff Norm called in to cause trouble."

"We best have a code word," Betty said, tapping her finger on her chin in thought. "Don't you step a foot out here unless you hear me say peaches. Otherwise I've got it all under control."

"The only problem with that is you *always* think you have it under control." Simpson took a seat on the bench chair at the breakfast nook and looked out the window at the sleek blue car that pulled to a stop.

She stepped out onto the porch and perched her hands high on her hips not looking overly welcoming. Out of the car stepped a tall familiar-looking man with a limp in his step and a look of unease in his eyes. There was a nervousness coursing through his whole body that Simpson could see even from this distance. A jumpy stranger was never a good surprise in his experience.

"Good afternoon, ma'am. I'm sorry to come up on you unannounced." The man pulled his hat from his head and dipped his chin in a greeting that looked half like an apology for the intrusion and half like a hello.

"I don't mind unexpected guests as long as they come with friendly hearts," Betty sang, and Simpson was in awe of her soft heart. With everything going on she was still willing to be kind first and ask questions later. "Oh my word." Betty clutched her chest as the man stepped closer, and she had a chance to view him straight on. "Nicky Grafton?"

Simpson's heart thudded so rapidly he worried they might hear it all the way from the porch. This was his brother, just ten feet from him. While most people would be excited, all he felt was fear. Nicky was a menace, no better than their father when it came right down to it, and he must have been the one Norm called in for backup on blocking the memorial and causing trouble. He didn't care if Betty intended to say peaches or not, he wasn't leaving her out there alone with the man who'd terrorized them both. When he stood to race out to the porch he was stopped by the gentleness in the man's voice.

"No, ma'am, I'm not Nicky. I'm Thomas Grafton, though I'm told pretty often I'm the spitting image of Nick. It's not much of a compliment. It just means I have the same big nose and chubby face."

"Little Tommy," Betty exclaimed, and Simpson watched her shoulders relax.

"That's what they used to call me. I do try to go by Thomas now. I am very sorry to intrude on you like this. It must be quite strange to have someone showing up here out of the blue. If you have a minute I'd like to explain what brings me out."

"Of course," Betty agreed, gesturing over to a chair on the porch and taking her place in her rocking chair.

"I got a phone call from a man last week about some goings on here in Edenville. He said I would be particularly interested in this and I should come as the memorial plans are set to be shared this coming Saturday."

"The man was named Norm?" Betty asked, and Simpson changed his position so he could keep from being seen all while analyzing his little brother's face and how it had changed over the decades.

"Yes, that was his name. When I came into town to meet him today I realized how badly we misjudged each other and something had been lost in communication. On the phone he was talking about how I should be here as a show of loyalty to my family. I'd assumed he meant to honor Simpson, he being my brother and all. At our meeting this morning I realized he meant my loyalty should be toward the preservation of the memory of my parents and their legacy. I'll tell you, our lunch didn't last long. After I went back to my hotel I started thinking about what he'd told me. He mentioned your involvement in the memorial, and I'll be honest, I was waylaid with old guilt."

"Guilt?" Betty asked.

"Yes, you are my brother Stan's widow. I should have been here when you lost Stan. I should have kept in touch with you. It feels wrong to make excuses." Simpson's heart ached as his brother blushed with remorse and embarrassment.

"There's a difference between excuses and explaining. I'd like to hear all you have to say." Betty crossed her legs and rested her hands in her lap, looking ready for a long chat.

"When Simpson was killed my mother and father left town, and me being young, I had to go with them. Stan stayed behind, and in their eyes that made him the enemy. I wanted to keep in touch, but after my brother Gary shipped off to Vietnam it was just me and my folks, and having my own convictions didn't seem like an option. Simpson had always told me to stay busy and out of the way, so that's what I tried to do. It meant cutting Stan out of my life while my parents were living, but, even after they were dead, it felt too hard to reconnect. I got married and had two daughters, and all I ever wanted was to insulate them from the childhood I had, from the knowledge of the twisted limbs on their family tree. But today, listening to what you're trying to do to honor my brother, I realize my daughters would be lucky to know you and call you their aunt. I only wish I'd done it sooner."

"My daughter grew up much the same way," Betty admitted. "The phone works both ways. I could have called you too. I understand what it's like to want to keep your children in a bubble. I was never quite sure where each of Stan's brothers stood on certain matters, and it was easier not to take the risk of trying to find out. I know for my daughter, Jules, to be able to meet some cousins of hers would be a dream come true. I'm glad you made the trip out here today. I'm only sorry about the pretenses Norm used to drag you to town."

"About the memorial, I want you to know my daughters and my wife are here in town with me too, and we will do whatever is

139

needed to help. I'm finally ready to share this part of my childhood with them, and I'm so glad it can be through something positive, even if the reality it's based upon is so dark. You just say the word and we'll be there, helping however is needed."

"That's so kind of you," Betty sang, reaching her hand out and touching Thomas's arm gently. "How long will you be in town?"

Thomas let out a little chuckle. "It's funny really, but we may be here quite a while. Both our daughters go to school in Virginia, and my wife and I sold our house last month with the intention of finding something on the east coast. I heard this morning in the coffee shop that our old farmhouse is set to be demolished soon. My wife, Ava, and I are considering buying it, as crazy as that sounds. It's hard for me to explain why I'd even consider something like that. You don't need me sitting here gushing about all my plans though."

"Like I said, I've got nowhere to be and explaining never hurts." Betty's voice was cool and welcoming, and Simpson knew full well the extra explanation was as much for his benefit as hers. She knew he'd want to hear as much as he could, considering he wouldn't be able to see his brother for himself.

Thomas swallowed hard and cleared his throat. Emotion was bubbling up to the surface as his cracking voice gripped for traction. "I'm the last of my brothers," Thomas explained. "You seem to have known Nicky, right?"

Betty let out a sarcastic snicker. "When I was a little girl he came up on me in a shack where I was playing with my friend who happened to be black. He attacked us and chopped my hair off practically down to the scalp. That explains why when I saw you walking up I probably looked as white as warm milk on a Sunday night. I flashed right back to that day."

The memory bowled Simpson over like a tidal wave. It was a defining moment that changed Betty, and he'd done nothing to stop it. Never in his life had he ever felt like such a coward and a failure. Never had he hated the blood he shared with his brother more.

"I'm so sorry for all the pain my family caused you." Thomas closed his eyes and shook his head. Obviously sharing Simpson's painful shame. "I'm sure you were still plenty pretty with short hair," Thomas replied, and when his face broke into a smile Simpson was transported back in time. The wrinkle at the bridge of his brother's nose and the way he raised one eyebrow higher than the other hadn't changed at all over the years.

"You're as charming as Stan ever was," Betty laughed. "I'm just glad those days have gone by. My life now is exactly how I always hoped it would be. I don't hold any hate about it. A good friend of mine used to say it's a whole lot easier to carry a tune than a grudge."

"As longs as you sing better than I do, I suppose. Simpson used to always say I sounded like a bullfrog with laryngitis when we had to sing hymns at church."

Simpson thought back to those Sunday mornings full of itchy shirts and what felt like endless lectures from the pulpit. But there were always a few moments of giddy laughter when Tommy or Stan would do something to get in trouble.

The little jovial twinkle in Thomas's eyes extinguished quickly as he began to speak again. "Nicky died three months ago from complications with his diabetes. He was so stubborn about taking his meds and going to doctor appointments. He was stubborn about everything really. As much as Nicky and I disagreed on a lot of things, it was still hard realizing I was the last man standing in my family. I know what kind of legacy most of my kin left in Edenville. It sounds like, with the exception of you and Stan, the Grafton name doesn't draw much positive reaction. Maybe I can help change that. Maybe Ava and my girls can help leave a different legacy here." Thomas dropped his hands into his lap and drooped his head slightly. "I missed a lot of opportunities to do the right thing. I kept quiet during plenty of kitchen table debates and stood by when I knew my family had done wrong. I'd convinced myself I wasn't going to trade my peace for the victory of pointing out my family's shortcomings. I believed lack of character always flushed itself out in time, and it did. I didn't need to be blowing the trumpet and calling them all fools; they proved they were again and again. But now that they're gone it's not the life I want to live anymore. Maybe coming back here will be an uphill battle but I'd rather be fighting than staying quiet anymore."

Simpson gave in to the tear that had formed in the corner of his eye and let it roll down his cheek. His tear ducts never got much of a workout over the years. But in the last decade they'd seemed to be trying to make up for lost time. Maybe it was his age, his understanding of mortality that made him quicker to give in to emotion. There was just something so nostalgic about listening to the way his brother spoke. Thomas always had a simple innocence about him, and it was still there, shining through.

"So you'll be joining us tomorrow for the unveiling of the plans for the memorial and the groundbreaking ceremony?" Betty asked, rocking casually in her chair.

"I wouldn't miss it. Ava and my girls will be there too, and I know they'll be excited to meet you and your daughter. Do you have much extended family that might be there?"

"We're a pretty big and imposing group, actually, but once you get over the noise and commotion we're a hoot to be around. I'm just sorry I can't invite you in tonight," Betty started and Simpson wondered what reason she'd come up with. "We're having some work done in the house, and it's not presentable."

"I understand. I should be on my way," Thomas said, reluctantly rising up from his chair and strolling slowly toward the steps. "I can't tell you what it means to me that you're so easy to forgive and so quick to welcome us. With Nicky dying and both my daughters now off to college, I was starting to feel very alone. Don't get me wrong, we go to a great church, and we have friends, but it's different to wake up one morning and feel like you have no family. There is something special about having someone who looks like you or remembers that train you got for Christmas when you were five. I've got Ava, and she's the best thing that ever happened to me, but there's nothing quite like having brothers. I even miss the bad ones."

Simpson knew exactly what that felt like. There was something about being one of eight boys. Even when it was ugly, even when you said you hated each other and had polar opposite beliefs, there was still a bond that couldn't be explained. The way Thomas was feeling right now, the isolation and the sense of being disconnected from something you'd always been tethered to, was life altering.

"I'm sure wherever they are, no matter what they did in this world, they're missing you too." Betty stood and hugged Thomas, and Simpsons wished it was his arms wrapping around his solemn-faced brother.

"Take care," he heard Betty call. Peering his head toward the front yard, he saw Thomas opening his car door to leave.

"Wait," he murmured in a hushed whisper that obviously couldn't be heard outside. "Wait," he called louder and then louder again as he shoved his way out the screen door. "Tommy, don't go."

Betty grabbed at Simpson's arm, but he shook her off and bolted down the stairs toward his brother. "It's me," he announced, clutching Thomas's shoulders and looking him square in the eye.

"Simpson?" Thomas choked out, stumbling backward, away from Simpson's hold as though he were escaping the grip of a ghost. "You're dead," he stammered, clutching his heart as his eyes went so wide they looked like they might pop out of his head.

"I'm not. I survived. You're not the last one standing. I'm here with you, brother. I'm here."

Thomas looked up at the porch for some kind of acknowledgment from Betty that he wasn't seeing things, that his brother was truly alive. When she brushed the tears from her cheeks and nodded her head, Thomas was overcome. Like a tree that had just been axed, his legs gave way and his knees hit the dirt. In an instant Simpson was down on his level, planting his own knees down on the ground and pulling his brother into his arms. "I'm alive," Simpson repeated over and over again as he squeezed his brother tightly. "I'm alive."

CHAPTER 18

The irony in telling Thomas he was alive was in how true it felt at that moment. He wasn't just saying that his body had life, that he hadn't been killed, but that for the first time in so long he felt the exhilaration of life coursing through him. That moment, crying with his brother as they knelt in the driveway, was the epitome of what living should feel like.

Betty came back onto the porch with a tray in hand and set it down between Thomas and Simpson, insisting they drink some coffee or tea to try to settle their nerves. "Should I leave you two alone?" she asked, the shadow of tears still in her red-rimmed eyes.

"Please stay," Simpson insisted, gesturing for her to sit with them. "This story belongs to all of us. We all had to live it."

Thomas sat shaking his head, his eyes fixed firmly on Simpson as if the idea of looking away were too scary. Perhaps Simpson would disappear like a puff of smoke in the wind if not watched closely. "I still can't believe this. It's been over forty years. Where have you been?"

"I survived that night, and Nate came up to the school and found me. They mended me up the best they could, and when they left town I went with them. I knew if I stayed my life would be over in one way or another anyway. We ended up settling in Arizona, and I fell in love with their daughter, Alma. I signed up for the Army and got very lucky with a few of my posts. They were remote and gave Alma and me a lot of freedom to be happy together." Simpson's words spilled out like rain from a cloud. His excitement was too much to contain, much like the smile on his face.

"Why didn't you ever contact me?" Thomas asked, the hurt dancing at the corners of his eyes.

"For a long time it wasn't safe for me to do that. Then life just moved so quickly. I was living under this new identity, and I couldn't risk exposing that. I had a wife and kids, and they were counting on me. But I wrestled with it, I want you to know that; every day I worried I'd made the wrong choice about not trying to find you." Simpson's words came out with a quiver, and it instantly sent Thomas into action.

"It's all right. I'm not blaming you," he assured him as he grabbed Simpson's arm and squeezed it firmly. "You had no choice but to run. I won't judge how you had to live your life as a result. I'm just sorry for the time we missed together. But that can end today. I'll call Ava and the girls and we can all go to dinner. They'll be over the moon to meet you."

Betty cleared her throat and nudged Simpson with her elbow. "Go on and tell him."

"Tell me what?" Thomas asked, looking terrified that this was still too good to be true. "What don't I know?"

"You can't tell your family about me just yet," Simpson explained apologetically. "I know that's a lot to ask, but it's complicated right now. If people were to find out I was alive there would be some trouble."

"I don't understand, what kind of trouble?" Thomas asked, looking unable to accept what was being said. "I've done well in the oil industry; I have some money. I can get you out of whatever problems you have."

"That's so generous of you, but I don't think money would help. Believe it or not I'm the criminal in all of this. After I left town I began living under an assumed identity. I purchased false documents and used them to enlist and get married. I've gotten some legal advice, and there is no way to really navigate the problems I'd have if people found out. They just all stack up on top of each other like a rotten onion, one bad layer after another."

"I don't want to keep this from my family. They wouldn't tell a soul if I asked them not to. I understand you don't know them and it's a risk, but please trust me." Thomas sounded desperate as he made a case Simpson could absolutely empathize with. Keeping secrets when the news was so powerfully exciting was like turning the handle on a jack-in-the-box right until the last beat and then stopping.

Simpson hung his head and thought through how different things would be after tomorrow. Would it really make a difference if he told his brother it was fine to tell his family? "I suppose you're right," Simpson said with a loving smile. "It can't hurt to just tell them. I'd appreciate it going no further though."

"Of course," Thomas agreed, nodding his head vehemently. "I swear it." Just like they did as boys he took two fingers and placed them over his heart. And like muscle memory taking over, Simpson did the same. Two old men just crossing their hearts like boys. "They'll want to meet you. Will you be at the ground-breaking ceremony tomorrow?"

"I won't be," Simpson said. "I'm not sure who else Norm has called in and what ties they might have had here in Edenville back in the day. I've mostly been staying here at the house so I won't be recognized on the off chance anyone figures it out. It's too risky."

"I understand," Thomas said glumly. "Norm did mention,

before he realized where my loyalties lie, that he'd contacted a few old Klan buddies of his daddy. He didn't say much other than he'd called them, and they were happy to come. They were rolling into town this afternoon. Not sure what to expect from them, but I want you to know I'm here for this. I'm not backing down no matter what. I'm not a crybaby little boy anymore. I'm with you. All of you."

"You were never a crybaby anymore than I was a real giraffe. Daddy gave us those names because he wanted to remind us he was the boss, he decided what we were called every day. You were a little boy in a scary time, and you were supposed to cry. We all should have been crying." Simpson clutched Thomas's shoulder and insisted he accept his words.

"I'm all in for this," Thomas said again. "But don't make me cry again. You'll undermine your point."

Betty's face lit with love as she looked fondly between the two men. "We're so happy to have you in our corner," she sighed. "To know you were both together again—I'm sure it's what Alma would have hoped for."

At the sound of his wife's name, Simpson felt a pang of guilt. It was impossible to know anymore what Alma would have wanted out of him, and that was part of the problem. He wished she'd have left him a road map to tell him what to do. But he was at peace with his choice now, and all he could do was pray she would have been as well.

"Are you hungry?" Simpson asked, hoping he'd be forgiven for the less-than-smooth change of subject.

"I am," Thomas laughed. "They've got some fair barbeque out in Texas, but I'll be honest, I've missed some good old North Carolina grub. I heard there is a great restaurant in town. My daughters looked it up on some rating thing on their phone and said it was the best. The Wise Owl, I think."

"No need," Simpson chuckled. "That's Betty's place.

Anything they have there is straight out of her own kitchen. As long as she doesn't mind making something."

"I'd be happy to," Betty said, hopping to her feet and clapping her hands together. "It's no trouble at all. I've always got something ready just in case."

"Just in case one of your long lost brothers-in-law shows up at your doorstep?" Thomas teased.

"Well laugh all you want, but so far it's happened twice this month. Always good to keep a chicken on hand just in case."

"She's great," Thomas smiled when Betty disappeared into the house and began clanking pots and pans around. "I'm glad Stan had her for the time he did. I'm sure she made his life better. When the rest of us left without him, and well, without you too, I couldn't figure out which way was up. I felt like everything had been fractured. It took a long time to feel put back together. It makes me feel better to know that if Stan was feeling that way too, he had Betty."

"She's the best. Stan was lucky to have her. Being here is the only thing that's gotten me through losing Alma. Betty's family is uniquely qualified to deal with pigheaded stubborn fools like me. I think you'll get on with them well. It helps to know you'll all have each other."

"And we'll have you too, right?" Thomas asked, fear filling his face. "You aren't going anywhere I hope. I just found you again. I'm not ready to lose you."

"Don't worry about that," Simpson said, trying to sound noncommittal but still comforting. "All you have to worry about now is what you'll do when you taste Betty's fried chicken. You'll never be the same."

CHAPTER 19

Simpson hadn't ventured out much in town, and not at all by himself, so he could feel his nerves raging as he knocked on the hotel room door. Around every corner he worried he might spot a Klan member in a hood holding a can of gasoline. In this day and age it wasn't all that likely, but his fear of Edenville was stuck somewhere in his adolescence, and the images were still painfully clear.

"Oh," Marline said, sounding surprised to see him there. "I wasn't expecting any company. My sister and I were just talking about the ceremony this afternoon. Are you here about that?"

"No," Simpson replied, staring down at his shoes. "I have to ask you a favor."

"Sir, if this is about reopening the case, I'm afraid we can't be swayed. I heard your family's arguments the other day. This is something we've been waiting our whole lives to do, and if we can't get justice then we at least want to shine a light on what really happened. We won't be persuaded otherwise."

"It's not about the case," Simpson assured her, and she stepped aside so he could come in. "Thank you. This is about that night at the school. There is something I want to tell you both."

"Aren't you from New York or something? Friends with Betty's husband?" April asked, looking at her sister in confusion. "What would you know about something that happened here four decades ago?"

"I know it all," Simpson admitted. "My name is actually Simpson Grafton. I was born and raised in Edenville and was at the school the night your mother was killed. I was right next to her as a matter of fact. I've had to keep this secret for many years and thought I'd take it to my grave, but you girls deserve the truth. You said you wanted to understand what happened, and I have the answers for you, but I need something in return."

"Our promise to keep your secret?" Marline asked, folding her arms over her chest. She was a fierce woman with sharp features and a brow that seemed to be able to tell an angry story. "You know I am a lawyer, and any information that comes to light about this case would help drive the trial. I can't promise you that."

"No, that's not what I'd like in return. As a matter of fact, the secret won't matter much in a little while. You're free to do whatever you like with the information I give you. But in return I need you to take these," Simpson said, pulling a stack of envelopes out of his coat and handing them to Marline, who received them reluctantly.

"What are they?" she asked, her lawyer instincts kicking in and telling her something about this was probably not legal.

"Over the years my wife, who was also from Edenville, kept in touch with Betty through those letters. In there is enough information to incriminate Betty on fraud and conspiracy charges regarding my false identity. I don't want them to fall into the wrong hands."

Marline placed them on the table as though wanting no part in holding something illegal. "Why not just burn them?"

"That's the only tie Betty has to my late wife and destroying

DANIELLE STEWART

them would be unthinkably cruel. I'd like her to have them back one day when it's safe."

Marline shook her head, seeming unconvinced, but April stepped forward and took the letters from the table. "Of course we'll do that. There's no harm in it."

"Not exactly," Marline interjected. "It could be considered obstruction of justice if we did."

"It could also be considered selfish if we didn't. It's the Christian thing to do, and if you are worried about the law then I'll do it myself," April said defiantly.

"No," Marline acquiesced. "I'll help find a place for them and get them back to Betty when the time is right. Now how about your end of the bargain?"

"Yes, you'd like to hear about your mother." Simpson took the offered seat in the chair by the window and looked out over the courtyard of the hotel. For the next half hour he explained to April and Marline how the tension at the school had come to a boiling point and how their mother, Ellie, had bravely protected others in the attack, giving children the chance to escape.

The girls held hands and cried as they heard of the horrors and heroism of that horrible day. "How is it that you survived?" Marline asked, her mouth agape with shock at the story she'd just been told.

"I'm not sure exactly. When Winnie ran home I was only able to fend off the guys attacking me for a minute or two, then they really started hammering me. It all went black, and I don't know what happened from there. The next thing I knew I was waking up on Winnie's kitchen table while a friend of theirs who was a nurse tried to stitch up the worst of my wounds. Nate got me out of there somehow."

"That's incredible," April said, her voice shaking with emotion. "You have to tell people this story. You may even be able to help get the case reopened. Who better than you to be able to tell us who was there that night?"

"He can't," Marline said knowingly. "Even if his intentions were good he'd face a mountain of litigation. But since he brought us those letters to protect his friend, I'm guessing he already knows that."

"I do," Simpson nodded. "But I might have one more thing that can help you. He pulled out the small journal he'd dug out from the floorboards of his childhood home and flipped through the pages. "This is a ledger. Unfortunately it does not include records of what happened that night because I stole it before then. But you will find the names of the local Klan members, crimes they were associated with, and what their ranks were. It's unlikely you'd find any of them alive or that this book would be enough to convict anyone, but at least it's a start."

"It's more than a start," Marline said. Unlike the letters, she was more than willing to snatch this gem from his hands. "I heard the Klan kept these but didn't think it would be possible to find one."

"You should know I made a copy. I have one more person who needs to see this before . . ." he trailed off, realizing that his plan was not yet public enough to elaborate any further. "I wish you both all the luck in the world with the case. Whether or not it is reopened and however it turns out, you should know your mother was a brave woman, and it seems she's passed that along to both of you."

The tears began again as Simpson stood to leave, not wanting to be pulled into the typhoon of feelings that were flowing. He wanted to give them time alone before the ceremony, and he had one more stop to make himself. "We'll be at the ceremony when it starts in a few hours. I'm sorry you can't be there. I'll walk with you to the lobby," Marline insisted as she followed him out the door.

When they hit the elevator she stopped him, looking back to make sure no one was listening. "You're in a tight spot, Simpson," she whispered. "I wish there was some legal advice I could give you, but I don't think there is. It seems very brave of you—a significant risk—to come here today. To tell me anything would be a gamble. But for some reason I'm looking at you and seeing a man who isn't very worried. I can't imagine a scenario that would either keep your secrets concealed once they come to light or protect you once you're exposed. If I were you, I'd be pretty troubled by that."

"When you live as long as I have and the way I've had to, not much troubles you. You have to accept that so much is outside of your control. All you can do is try your best. I can't waste time on worry." The doors to the elevator opened and the bell chimed.

"You have a funny look in your eyes. Are you sure you're all right?" Marline asked as he stepped in and the doors began to close. He offered nothing back in the way of an answer as the steel came together in front of him. He wasn't all right, but in a few hours the conflict raging inside him would be over.

CHAPTER 20

Pulling open the heavy oak door to Calhoon's bar, Simpson held his breath against the cloud of cigarette smoke that enveloped him. It was a dark, windowless bar with a sticky floor and flickering static-filled old televisions in every corner.

The place was practically deserted but for a distracted female bartender talking on her cell phone and a lone figure bellied up to the bar. Judging by his slumped shoulders and the stack of empty bottles in front of him, Norm wasn't in a good state of mind. Simpson would have to tread lightly.

"Sorry to interrupt." Simpson pulled out the stool next to Norm and took a seat. "I'll have a water," he said to the bartender, who never looked up from her phone.

"What the hell are you doing here?" Norm hissed before swigging back the last sip of his amber beer and slamming the bottle down a centimeter from Simpson's hand.

"I didn't think you'd be alone," Simpson said, turning his stool so he could get a better look at Norm and the disheveled state he was in. "I figured you and your crew would be getting ready to make a stink down at the ceremony later today."

"I'm alone," Norm grunted. "I'm alone in this."

"I heard through the grapevine you'd called up some old Klan members, friends of your father's, and they'd agreed to come to Edenville." Simpson nodded his head in gratitude as the waitress brought over his water, but she didn't notice.

"They came," Norm explained, gesturing for the waitress to crack open another beer for him. "Apparently they go to different parts of the South now and do speaking engagements. They came here to talk to me about the past and how it can help shape the future, blah blah blah. No one understood why I was asking them here, or if they did, they decided to come and downright counter what I'm trying to do." He moved his hands animatedly and knocked over an empty bottle that Simpson quickly caught.

"Maybe they'd be worth listening to," Simpson said, moving all the beer bottles a few inches farther from Norm's flailing arms.

"Then listen to them when they speak today at the ceremony. They were nice enough to offer up their services. I kicked them off my front porch. Traitors."

"Have you ever thought of it more as an evolution? People can change their minds and their ideas on things. I don't really believe you to be a racist, but I can't for the life of me understand why you want to cause so much trouble." Simpson leaned back as Norm spun, quickly pointing a finger just inches from his nose.

"I am not a racist," Norm growled. "Neither was my daddy; all he was trying to do was protect this town and his family. He had pride, just the same as I do. Everyone here was poor, and the white folks couldn't go splitting what little they had with people coming in to steal their jobs and flood their schools. He didn't want any harm to come to anyone, but he was doing it for me. Then people came into this town—reporters, lawyers, and politicians—and they played pin the tail on the Klan."

"Sounds like a terrible party game," Simpson chuckled, trying to lighten the mood unsuccessfully.

"Those people, just like you, are outsiders, and they think

there is just one side to the story. They think it was just evil men doing evil things."

Simpson pulled the large envelope from under his arm and laid it on the bar. "Some of them were, Norm. I'm not painting with a broad-brush here, I understand that some folks didn't mean any harm, but a good majority of the Klan wanted blood. And they got it right here in the place you've lived your whole life. I know you're trying to preserve your father's legacy, but you have to understand, those people out there are just trying to do the same for their kin. The plaque, the park they want to make, it means something to this town."

"You ain't even from here," Norm slurred. "Why do you care so much? I don't care if I'm alone in this. After my next beer I'm going to sleep this off in my truck for a couple hours and then go down to that ceremony, and I'm saying my piece. For my daddy."

"I want you to look at something." Simpson pulled the documents out of the envelope and held them in front of Norm. "This is a ledger of the Edenville Chapter of the Klan from the early 1960s. If you read it you'll see specifically what members did and to whom. You'll read about acts of extreme violence and how they viewed that as a success, often times resulting in an increase of rank for a member. These documents will have familiar names. You'll see your daddy's name in there, and you'll see things he did."

Norm slapped at Simpson's hand, trying unsuccessfully to knock the documents away. "How do I know you didn't just make these up?"

"You don't know, and if you convince yourself I did then that's what you'll believe. But if you stop for just a minute and really look at them, you'll realize they are real. And when you do, you'll see what the Klan did here. What you won't find on these pages are the reasons why they did the things they did. Maybe you're right about your daddy's motivation. But you're wrong in trying to call anything he did justified. The daughters of Ellie Perry are in town, and they want justice for the murder of their mother. They'll get the case reopened, I'm sure, and in that process you'll hear what really happened that night at the school. Your father's story will be debunked, and even if there is no one left to prosecute, the truth will be brought to light. Don't wait for that moment. Get there on your own."

"You mean admit my father was a liar? That he filled my head with garbage, and everything I believe is wrong?"

"Don't you see the absolute message in your daddy's lie? He told you a softer version of the story because he didn't want you to see him as a killer or a hate-mongering monster. Changing the story shows he held some guilt, some remorse for what had happened, and he wanted to preserve your image of him. He cared what you thought, and he didn't want to lose that. Let it count for something, but don't let it hold you in this dark place. I think in your heart you know the truth."

"I think you're a nosy out-of-town jerk who is just hell-bent on persecuting people," Norm hissed, snatching the papers from Simpson's hands and ripping them in half. "I think if my daddy were here today he'd pull your ass outside and beat you upside your head."

Simpson thought on that for a moment. There was a good likelihood that Norm's dad had already beat Simpson up forty years ago. It made his mouth curl into a smile even though the situation didn't call for it. The irony was just too much to deal with.

"Well, I won't be your problem much longer," Simpson announced as he stood and tipped his chin to Norm.

"Good," Norm bit back, throwing the stack of now ripped papers to the floor. "Take that bitch Betty with you, too, before someone teaches her a lesson."

Simpson's hand was already on the door when those words hit

him in the back like a two-by-four. He released the cold brass from his palm, turned quickly, and backtracked. Grabbing a handful of what was left of the man's hair, he yanked Norm backward until he was practically balancing horizontally on the stool. "Do not underestimate the lengths to which I will go in order to keep that from happening. Do not misjudge my kind nature for weakness, because I can assure you, the day you cross Betty will be the last day you walk this earth. I was trying to be nice to you," Simpson growled, tugging a little harder. "Maybe when you sober up you'll smarten up."

Simpson shoved Norm back up to a sitting position and then dropped his heavy head on the bar. He didn't fight to sit back up, he just lay there with his drunk red cheek pressed against the cold bar and closed his eyes. Simpson had genuinely hoped this encounter would have gone better, but he was done allowing anyone to threaten or hurt Betty. He'd been powerless for so many years, then gone for even more. As long as he was here, he'd take a stand for her.

As he stepped out of Calhoon's and rounded the corner back toward Main Street, Simpson heard the chattering of people as they passed by. There was an excitement about the ceremony, and he was glad to hear it. Everyone was making plans for later that afternoon and discussing what they expected to hear and see.

He wouldn't lie and say he didn't wish things were different. It would be great to be able to partake in all the validation and joy that could come out of an afternoon like the one they were about to have, but that wasn't possible for him. He knew what he needed to do, and there was no more putting it off. Pulling one last envelope from his pocket with the name *Frankie* scrolled across the front, he headed for Betty's restaurant.

CHAPTER 21

Simpson sat in the woods adjacent to his old school and employed all his old military tactics to blend in. He'd come early, wanting some peace and quiet before the crowd gathered. Michael, who'd been working tirelessly, had done an amazing job. The land on which the school once resided had been plowed and cleared of all the overgrown grass and fallen limbs, leaving freshly turned earth looking ready for new life in its place. A podium stood on a recently erected small stage with a set of metal stairs leading up to it. Chairs were lined up row after row, a sign of how many people they were hoping to draw.

Off to the left of the podium was a large board that displayed the plans for the memorial. The sun shone down on it all, blessing it. Simpson sat through the microphone checks and the discussion of the order in which each guest speaker would be presented. Then finally it was time.

The crowd began filing in, hugs and handshakes flowing like water down a swollen creek. There was so much delight in the sea of diverse colors and ethnic backgrounds. If nothing else happened here today, Simpson found peace in this monumental moment—one that, as a young man, he never believed he would witness.

The speakers popped and fought static as they settled and came to life. "Thank you all so much for coming here today," Michael announced, hushing the chattering crowd. "The question has been posed, why is Michael Cooper, a man from Ohio, spending his money to make a memorial for something that happened years before he was born? I want to take this opportunity to answer. The complicated version is my mother-in-law, Betty, whom most everyone knows, was here that night. Recently, after many years of keeping it to herself, she sat our family down and told us the story of her youth, punctuating it with that night. Because, in reality, that was the last day of her childhood. That story touched me. But it was the way it seemed to impact my daughter that brought me here today." Michael gestured down at Frankie, who ducked her head in a sudden onset of bashfulness.

"When I saw these events through my child's eyes, I realized how important it would be to pay homage to those who died, give freedom to those who lived it to speak out and teach the next generation so we do not repeat the same mistakes. I want my daughter to be able to come to this place and ask questions. I want Betty to be able to sit on one of the benches below a shady tree and reflect. Today you'll hear from a very wide range of people. Some were impacted directly by the events on this sacred ground. Others never set foot in Edenville but understand the balance that comes from creating a legacy. We're honored to have them all with us today. First I'd like to welcome April and Marline Perry. They are the daughters of Ellie Perry, an African American teacher who worked at the school and lost her life here."

A roar of applause broke out as Michael welcomed the women to the stage. "Thank you," Marline started, and Simpson could tell she was beating back the tears. "My mother didn't lose her life here," Marline corrected. "That sounds too gentle. It was stolen from her. It's a dramatic and sensational way to say it, but it's also the truth. Someone stomped the life out of our mother right here, probably not far from where I stand. It would be easy for my sister and me to be bitter, and if I'm being honest, there is certainly some of that. But the emotion I felt the strongest was surprise when I found out about this memorial. These stories are rarely talked about. Not even by the families of the victims. It is easy to believe no one cares. My sister and I frequently assumed everyone in Edenville was still racist, that you were all racist back then. Receiving a phone call letting us know that someone we'd never met wanted to honor our mother was the wake-up call I needed. Making those assumptions says more about me than it does about anyone who lives here. My point is, talking about this helps. Giving this tiny space on the earth a label and a physical memorial means something. We need to name names, not just those who committed the crimes but those who were victims. We need to shine a light on history so we can finally lay it to rest.

"I understand the argument that we are dredging up the past. Forty years have gone by, why must we all apologize for something we didn't even do? And the answer to that is, because sometimes you should. Sometimes when the person next to you is heartbroken you should hug them and say you're sorry they are hurting. We are hurting. My sister and I are heartbroken, and in the coming months we will work to bring light to the dark corners of this case. When you see us, please remember our pain. When we ask you questions, please remember our purpose. We are not here to tarnish the town. On the contrary, we are here to help show how far it has come. All of you turning up here today, the smiles we see shining back at us, are a testament to that."

Simpson shifted on the stump he was sitting on and dropped his face into his hands. When you were going to do something as final as he was, it was almost impossible not to flip-flop back and forth on whether or not you'd made the right choice. He shook himself from the sea he was falling into and focused on the next person to take the stage.

"Many of you know," the woman said loudly, "I am the current superintendent of the Edenville public school system. I'm proud to be a part of a community that can come together for important things. When I heard about the idea for this memorial I began to research the events further and am embarrassed how little I knew about the history of the school system I represent today. I'm originally from Oregon, a transplant here in high school, and I loved it so much I came back after college. I couldn't believe the struggles that faced the African American teachers who bravely came to work at schools who, frankly, did not want them there. Or later years when the students began integrating the schools and the adversity they faced. I could not believe it," she said, emphasizing her last sentence and punctuating it with a long pause, "and that's when I realized I'm part of a generation of people who can't believe how hard it was. And because people bravely paved the way, I'll likely never have to navigate our schools through anything even remotely as volatile. Odds are our children will never encounter what their grandparents did. So to honor those who changed the course of history, the Edenville Public School Department would like to present honorary awards to Mr. Kole and Mrs. Ellie Perry from the National Council of Educators. Also included in that list are the six other teachers who first found the courage to teach under extraordinary circumstances. May their commitment, no matter the circumstances, inspire us all."

Included in that list, Simpson realized, was Winnie. It pained him to know she didn't live long enough to see this moment. Alma and Nate hadn't either. They'd become his family, and they'd all left him behind. Too anxious to sit for another minute, Simpson sprang to his feet and strode a few yards farther into the woods. He wanted the applause to sound far away. He wanted to be far away. Maybe it was time? Maybe he should just do it already. He drew in a deep breath, and then he heard it. Someone else had begun talking and a whisper in his ear told him to go back. He wouldn't want to miss this.

CHAPTER 22

With a cane in his hand and a wobble in his step, a man made his way to the microphone. Clearing his throat and flattening out a piece of folded paper, he readied himself to speak. "I was a member of the Edenville chapter of the KKK, and I was here the night of the murders." A hush fell over the crowd and Simpson angled himself to see if he could identify who the man was. When he couldn't place him, he turned his attention to the crowd where Betty and her family sat. Next to them were his brother, Thomas, and his wife, and their two pretty daughters. Their mouths had all fallen wide open as they looked at each other, hoping they'd heard wrong.

"I'm sure with that one statement y'all will form an opinion of me. But let me cast some doubt on that assessment and try to make a very important point. I was eleven years old. Always tall for my age, my father insisted it was never too early to make a man out of me. Like other people here, that night changed my life. In a way it wrecked it. For years after I was never the same, always getting in trouble and doing drugs. Anything to get those images out of my mind, but nothing worked until I started talking about it." The man hesitated and drew in a deep breath, seeming to forget the microphone was on. "I'm glad this case may be reopened, and I will personally assist in any way I can because I am sorry. Like the daughters of Ellie said, while I didn't lay a finger on anyone that night, it doesn't mean I can't apologize and mean it deeply. I am so very sorry any of this happened.

"There is just one point I'd like to make as this town begins to face the reality of history. It would be easy to lump every man in the Klan into the same category of hate. But I certainly didn't hate anyone. There were plenty of other men there that night who had no idea what had been planned. If they had, they never would have gone. I saw regret. I saw remorse, and I believe every story needs context. Every story needs multiple viewpoints. That night while I stood frozen by fear, certain images were etched in my mind. There are ones I won't repeat here because they already haunt me, no reason they should do so to all of you. But I will share some small moments of humanity. As I stood still, trying to see clearly through the holes in my too big hand-me-down white hood, I saw a Klan member lift a young woman who the crowd had surrounded, and he shouted for her to run."

Simpson looked out at Betty and watched her wipe at the corners of her eyes with a handkerchief. He knew she was the girl who'd been spared, saved by her father's reluctant act of mercy. Though it was fleeting and not broad enough to save any other lives that night, it still mattered.

"I saw the tallest and strongest man I'd ever seen pull his hood from his head and hit his knees, vomiting into the edge of the woods, overcome by the atrocities before him. I myself wet my pants and cried for my mother. There were plenty of us who didn't have the stomach for this, who wished we'd have known what was planned so we could be anywhere else.

"When most of the Klan had cleared out, a few remained and began pouring the gasoline. I still can't fill my car without that day coming right back to me. A moment that stands still in time for me is when one of the men leaned down and grabbed a life-less-looking body by the leg and yanked him a few feet from the rest of them. I heard him say, 'Giraffe, why did you have to be brave?' as he stepped back. It was such a strange thing to say; I knew I'd remember it my entire life.

"Then someone grabbed my arm and yanked me toward the woods. I've replayed all that night over and over in my mind many times. I want this story to be told; I think it's exactly what this world needs, and I can't wait to see it woven together. Thank you for allowing me to show there were many facets, many stories here, and they all deserve to be told."

Simpson began to hyperventilate, clutching at the log he was sitting on to keep himself from toppling over and hitting the ground. He'd wondered for years what type of fortune or guardian angel had kept him far enough away from those burning bodies to survive long enough for Nate to come find him. He'd imagined it a thousand ways, but he'd never once allowed himself to consider his father had a hand in it. That would undermine the evil he'd attached to the memory of his father, the unwavering malice and hate couldn't be real if he made an attempt to save him.

Feeling like he was losing his grip on the moment, he stood and stumbled a few steps farther into the woods until he found himself in a run. Ducking below branches and jumping over stones, he moved not like a man of his age, but the way he did as a boy navigating this very area. He ran until his legs burned and the cramping stitch in his side felt like it would split him in half. He wasn't exactly sure how far he'd run or even which direction he'd gone. But he could no longer hear the applause or chatter from the ceremony.

"Why, Daddy?" he called up to the clouds as he hit his knees. "Why didn't you just let me die? Why didn't you leave me there?" Simpson leaned backward, laying his head on a pile of leaves and staring at the trees and sky as gravity pulled tears down the sides of his face toward his ears. It was time.

Bringing his hand up to his lips he blew a kiss out toward the sky and prayed the wind would carry it to Alma.

BETTY WISHED SO BADLY that Simpson had been here to witness the incredible things unfolding at the ceremony today. The biggest of which was the revelation that his father may have saved his life. She knew from personal experience the conflict that stirred inside of a person, but it was always better to know.

Her handkerchief was soaked now, and all she could think of was racing back to her house to share everything with Simpson. He was the first person she knew whose situation seemed beyond repair. His pain couldn't be fixed with home-cooking and long talks. There were so many years of it stacked up on him she just wasn't sure he'd ever be completely out from under it. But maybe with time. That's what she kept telling herself. Sure, there was the legal aspect of it all and the danger of him being found out if he stayed in town. But wasn't there something to be said for just being around people who loved you? Didn't that mean anything?

As the church choir moved to the front of the crowd to start a song, Betty felt a frantic tap on her shoulder. Turning around she saw Megan, the hostess from the restaurant, crouched down and looking white as a ghost. "I'm so sorry to bother you, Betty."

"Did the place burn down or something because you look like you're about to pop out of your skin," Betty asked in a hushed voice, trying not to draw too much attention to herself.

"No, the restaurant is fine," Megan said hurriedly, still trying to catch her breath.

"Then maybe this can wait until after. You're interrupting the singing." Betty gestured back up toward the front and tried to crouch down so the staring eyes couldn't keep landing on her.

"I know you always call me nosy, and I should stop it. Sometimes it's a bad thing but other times it's been a good thing." Megan's breathless whisper was loud enough to have many heads turning their way.

"Girl, if you don't spit it out already I'm gonna knock you down and pretend I don't know you. What's the matter?"

"Clay's friend—he came by and dropped off a note with Frankie's name on it. You had told me you were a bit worried about him and that's why you've been spending more time at home. He had this funny look in his eye and something just felt weird, so I read the note."

"Seriously, girl, I don't know how you keep track of your face the way your nose is always poking in everyone else's business." Betty glared at Megan as a few people began to try to hush them.

"Read it," Megan said, dropping the note in Betty's lap. "I think he's going to do something bad. I think he might hurt himself."

Betty frantically unfolded the paper and read it.

DEAR FRANKIE,

I KNOW you have forty-one questions left for me, but I won't be able to answer them. It's unfair. That's something you'll encounter for the rest of your life; I'm just sorry to be the first to let you down. You might not understand my choice today. Maybe you never will, but know that I am at peace with it. This is what I want. That might not be enough to keep you from being angry, but someday you might come to understand.

Meeting you was a blessing. Every now and then gifts pop up

in your life when you least expect them. I consider you to be one. Forgive me.

SIMPSON.

BETTY YELPED as she jumped to her feet and grabbed Bobby's arm for him to follow. Stepping over bags and landing on people's poor toes, they hurdled their way to the edge of the row.

"What's the matter?" Bobby asked, not slowing his pace to insist she explain herself. She was glad that over the years they'd all grown to understand if Betty is running you best be running too.

"It's Simpson. I think he's going to hurt himself. He left a note for Frankie, and it sounded very final."

"Maybe he's just planning to leave." Bobby snatched the note from Betty's hand and read it as they hustled to the back of the field where all the cars were parked. "Damn," Bobby sighed.

"I know," Betty replied, clutching her heart. "Where could he be? The woods you think? That day he cut his wrist and I found him, maybe he'd go back there? We have to stop him. I'll never forgive myself if I lose him. Not this way."

"I'll round up some on-duty officers and have them start looking for him. Michael and I can head into the woods, and maybe you and Piper go back to the house. There's a chance he's there. Make sure Jules keeps the kids away though. I don't want them to—" As Bobby struggled to finish his thought, the choir's song came to a close, and a voice came over the microphone. It was low at first, but enough to stop both he and Betty in their tracks. "I don't think he was going to hurt himself," Bobby said, pointing up at the podium where Simpson stood. "I think he's going to turn himself in."

CHAPTER 23

Simpson hesitated, feeling much less comfortable than he thought he would now that everyone's eyes were on him. He watched silently as Bobby and Betty made their way back from the parking area and toward the front where they had been sitting. Betty made a move to keep coming, but he nodded slightly, letting her know he was fine and she should sit.

"I-um, I know you all thought the last speaker would be the last one, but I, um, hope you'll all stay a few more minutes so I can share something with you." The faces staring back at him were mostly unfamiliar and looked pretty confused. So he tuned them out and focused only on the few people at the front of the crowd who were staring at him with joy and love. That was what would carry him through this. "For the last forty-something years I've gone by the name S McKinney. You don't need a very keen eye; even you folks in the back can tell I'm well over forty years old. Math doesn't lie, but people do. I'm sorry, this is very difficult for me," Simpson said, swallowing hard and clutching the podium for dear life. "My name for the first eighteen years of my life was Simpson Grafton. A name you'll see if you look closely at the plans for this memorial. I was here the night of the attack, and I was thought to have been killed, but I survived. The man who was up here before me spoke of a Klan member pulling a lifeless body a few feet from the burning ones. Though I wasn't conscious, I believe that was my father trying to spare me. Where I went from there, what my life turned into, doesn't really matter. All that matters is what brought me to this podium today." Simpson drew in a deep breath and then flashed a smile down at Frankie who was clutching her father's arm nervously.

"I know there are people attending today who will have to act on this information: police officers, lawyers, judges. I'm well aware of the legal implications I'll be facing, considering I lived more than half my life under a false identity. This is a choice I'm making because I've hidden too long. Every day I wasn't myself was a day I was dishonoring what happened in Edenville. I should have been here championing this type of memorial instead of pretending it never happened. But I'm inspired by the people who came here today and are doing just that. I'm inspired by you all. If two girls whose mother was killed can be brave enough to fight for justice, then I can stand here and tell the truth. If a man who once wore the hood can come here and explain and apologize, then I can stand here.

"It may not seem from the outside sometimes, but I've been overwhelmingly lucky in my life. I married a strong and beautiful woman, and we had two sons together. I had a great military career. Coming back to Edenville after all of that was difficult, but I was lucky enough to have people help me. Edenville is a great community. The past is far behind you all, and that was what I believe I needed to see before I could stand before you today and be honest. Whatever the consequences, I'm ready to face them. It's not about having to be my true self. It's just about standing here and speaking it out loud and making it real." Simpson accidently thumped the microphone as he went to wipe a bead of sweat from his brow. He stared down at the swirling oak of the podium, unable to glance up. Stunned silence filled in every crevice around him, and while he knew he'd made the right decision, he still felt overwhelmingly afraid.

When his eyes finally made a connection with the audience again he saw a man coming from the back in a police uniform. Surely they weren't going to put him in cuffs right here and drag him away in front of the crowd? The way Michael had explained it when the issue first came up was that there would be an investigation period and then charges would be filed. It seemed a bit extreme to just yank him off the stage and toss him in a cruiser.

As the officer climbed the stairs, Michael, Bobby, and Betty shot to their feet, but he waved them off. "As most of you here know, I'm Captain Eugene McCormick of the Edenville Police Department," the man said as he leaned in toward the microphone. Simpson backed up a few inches to give him space. "I'm sorry, Mr. McKinney," the captain said glancing at Simpson. "You'll have to forgive us small town folks. We don't have the same kind of technology you're probably used to where you're from in New York."

Simpson's face twisted in confusion and for a fleeting moment he wondered if he was having a stroke or something. What on earth was this man talking about? Why was this man calling him by his fake name still, and talking like he really believed he was from New York?

"You see," McCormick continued, adjusting the microphone slightly, "we were all trying to listen intently to you but just after you stepped up here this darn microphone must have gone on the fritz. I couldn't hear a thing you said; I don't think any of us could." He gestured out at the crowd, looking at them to speak up in agreement, and after a moment they did. People shouted, *couldn't hear a thing* and *not sure what he said.* "Things like that happen here in small towns, but I'm sure you can forgive us." He looked over at Simpson expectantly until he nodded he did indeed forgive them.

"What we lack in quality equipment we make up for in empathy and acceptance. That's really why everyone turned out here today. I hope that you, Mr. McKinney," the captain said, reiterating the use of Simpson's false identity, "enjoy your time here in Edenville. You are most welcome in this town, and we'd love to have you as long as you'd like to stay. It's true this town has old secrets, and we're looking to bring light to them. But every once in a great while you come across a secret that is best kept quiet, and there ain't no better place than a small town to do that." He turned and faced Simpson, extending his hand for a firm handshake that quickly turned into a hug.

"Thank you," Simpson managed as he patted the captain's back firmly. "You really think everyone is just going to—" Before he could get his question out, the captain spun him back around to face the crowd that was on its feet and cheering.

"They already have."

CHAPTER 24

"I think we may need to admit this tiny house just isn't big enough for our family anymore," Betty said, sliding into Clay's arms as she watched the caravan of cars pulling in for midweek dinner. "Now with Thomas, Ava, and Simpson coming over from their house every week, and Ray popping in when he's finished at school, we're going to have to start eating in two different rooms."

"We'll make do," Clay assured her, planting a kiss on the crown of her head. "I think everyone would rather be elbow to elbow here than have to eat anywhere else."

"Suppose you're right," Betty sighed as she waved to the kids who were barreling toward the porch. "Go on in and wash up. You'll be setting the table tonight. You each know your job."

Frankie lingered for a moment, not charging forward with the other kids. She was somewhere in the middle, too big for the little kids and too small to fit in with the adults. Betty could see she was spending a lot of time trying to find where she belonged lately.

Simpson stepped up and reached his hand out for a high five, which Frankie gladly gave him. "You've answered all one hundred of my questions," she reminded him. "That means you can go anytime you want."

"I guess we need a new deal then, don't we?" Simpson asked, tossing the ball back into her court with a raised eyebrow.

Frankie thought on it, pressing her finger to her chin. "Maybe you could ask me a hundred questions. Well no, never mind, that's dumb. I don't really have anything to talk about."

"I don't believe that for a second," Simpson shot back quickly. "I bet I could ask you two hundred questions and never get bored. Is the bus dropping you off here tomorrow?"

"If my mom says it's all right," Frankie shrugged, then smiled adding, "That's one, only one hundred ninety-nine to go!"

"You got me. I'll have my questions ready. No leaving town until I get through them all, you have to promise." Simpson's mouth curled into a playful smile as Frankie rolled her eyes.

"I'm too little to leave town," she huffed back as she turned and headed for the door to join the other kids inside. Betty caught an excited grin on Frankie's face as she passed, and she was grateful for his new agreement.

"She's taken a shine to you," Betty said, touching him affectionately on the shoulder. "I'm sorry I missed seeing you with your own boys when they were that age."

"They'd have liked to have you spoil them rotten back then. I called them yesterday, you know. It was hard, but I told them everything. They were shocked, but it seemed like each of them was coming around by the end of it. It's a lot to take in"

"When can you see them? They're welcome here any time; I hope you told them that. The house is small, but we always find room."

"They both get leave from their posts in about six months. My brother Thomas offered some space once they get settled in a place too. He actually offered a room to me as well." Simpson turned his eyes away as though his moving out would be some kind of slight against Betty's hospitality.

"That's wonderful," Betty cried as she slapped her hands together. "We'd miss you here, but I can't think of anything Alma would have wanted more for you than to reconnect with your brother. Just don't become a stranger around here."

"Betty I don't think anyone is a stranger to you, not for long anyway." He winked at her and headed back out to the driveway as everyone continued to arrive.

The chaos that ensued as people piled out of vehicles and exchanged hugs was louder than ever. They hung around the front yard and leaned against their cars as they laughed and teased each other. Thank goodness for the good weather or they'd be on top of each other in the house trying to talk over one another. Betty watched Simpson's profile as he told an old joke he'd been telling since they were kids, and like always he was unable to get the punch line out without cracking up.

When one more car came around the bend and up the driveway Betty couldn't imagine who else might be coming. She felt her stomach fill with rocks at the sight of Norm stepping out onto her driveway. They'd heard next to nothing from him since before the ceremony over a month ago, and she was glad for that. Everyone in town had welcomed Simpson with open arms, and Norm was the only person left she was worried might stir trouble. She shook out of Clay's arms and in a flash placed herself between Simpson and the approaching man.

"There's an awful lot of us here. You should have picked a different night if you wanted a fight." Betty lifted her chin defiantly and folded her arms across her chest, staring him down like an angry badger.

"No fight left in this dog," Norm replied sounding exhausted. "I just came here to talk to Simpson. I owe him an apology."

Betty's mouth opened to reply but snapped shut when she

couldn't think of any kind of suitable response. It didn't happen often, but Norm had genuinely silenced her with his shocking statement.

"Can you stay for dinner?" Simpson asked, stepping out from behind his shield that was Betty. "She's made enough stew for half the town."

"I can imagine not everyone would want to share a table with me. I couldn't blame them," Norm said, pulling his hat from his head and wringing it in his hands. "I've actually got a meeting to go to anyway. An AA meeting."

"That's good to hear," Michael interjected, clearly having to fight his better instincts and find a way to be nice. Even though the effort could be read on his face, it counted. He was still trying.

"It's just that I finally got around to reading those papers you brought me. After I taped them back together, that is. I didn't really need to see what they said to know I was wrong, but I'm still glad you brought them. I know you were trying to give me something to help me understand. Thank you."

"The things you've been living with," Simpson said quietly, "it's a real journey to find your way back, but you can do it. Just stick with it."

Norm's head rose up from his nervous hands, and his face read sheer surprise. "Why would you care how things turn out for me at this point? I was terrible to you."

"Nowadays people can change. Back then it wasn't easy for someone to turn their lives around and run in a new direction. Our fathers didn't have that luxury the same way you and I do. That's one of the nice things about the world now. You're different because you're working hard to understand things and make sense of them. I'm different because I'm happy to see you doing it. Neither of our fathers would have been able to do those things."

"I don't want to be like my daddy," Norm admitted. "That's a real hard thing for me to say, but it's true. I have to believe that even though he didn't know how to say it, he'd have wanted me to do better than he did. Maybe that's why he lied about how everything happened."

"I appreciate you coming out here," Simpson said. "And I know when you first heard who I really was you must have wanted to do something to get me punished for it. I appreciate that you didn't."

"The day I heard is the last day I took a drink and the first day in a long time I shed a tear. I'm not too proud to admit that. To know what you went through, to see you come back here and face this place again even with the sacrifice you'd have to make to do it, that's part of what started this change in me." Norm's eyes darted away, the honesty becoming too much for him. The group around him quieted so they could listen, unsettling him. "I best get going. The meeting is all the way in Rockport. It's a long way out."

"Why don't I come along?" Simpson offered with a casual shrug. "I'm sure two good ole boys like us with fathers like ours could have a whole lot to talk about on the ride."

"I, um, I don't know what to say," Norm admitted. "The company would be appreciated. Almost as much as your forgiveness is."

Norm planted his hat back on his head and gave a wave as he hopped into his car. Simpson hesitated, turning to look at Betty before he left. "You really do work magic," he whispered as he kissed her on the cheek.

"This isn't my doing. I didn't get him to stop drinking." Betty tossed her hands up like she was innocent of performing any magic at all.

"It's not how you made him change; it's how you helped me get to a place where I could accept it. Sorry is enough for me now. Happy is an option for me today. I couldn't have done that without you."

"I love you, Simpson. You're my brother. I just wish we hadn't lost forty years right in the middle of it all."

"If nothing's ever lost you don't get to experience the wonderment and joy of rediscovering it." Simpson shook a few hands and gave a few hugs as he got in the car with Norm.

Betty felt like laughing and crying all at the same time. She felt like screaming up to heaven with the improbable hope that Alma and Winnie could hear her. But she realized there was really only one thing she could do.

"Who's hungry?" she asked, waving her family into her tiny house. There were so many things in this world Betty couldn't do. She couldn't cure cancer to save her friend. She couldn't go back in time and undo all that had happened. But she could fill some bellies, and tonight that was just going to have to be good enough.

EPILOGUE

Eight years later (Frankie)

DEAR GRAMMY,

I KNOW you must consider this note the coward's way out. You're probably right. I knew if I stuck around long enough to tell you I was leaving, you'd have found a way to talk me out of it. I'm eighteen now and so no need to send the search party out and alert the police. I'm leaving by choice, and I know it's the right thing for me. Something's happened, and I need to go see it through.

The stories you've all told over the years are full of adventure and victories, and it's my time to start my own. College begins this fall, and I know once I go it'll be years before I have a chance at something like this again. I'll buckle down and focus on my grades and be the responsible person you've always taught me to be. I'm just not ready for that yet. Maybe once I put this to rest.

Please tell my mother I'm sorry for leaving without saying goodbye. Tell my father I will be safe, because he's taught me how. If it's possible, get Uncle Bobby to calm down and not call the National Guard in to rescue me. Ask Piper to be the voice of reason that she always is.

I promise I will be careful. Please promise you will trust me. I need to know you believe I'll be all right. Because then I will be.

LOVE ALWAYS,
   Frankie

CONTINUE The Edenville Series with Book 3, Stars in a Bottle

EXCERPT FROM STARS IN A BOTTLE

Frankie

Admitting I'm wrong is not an option. If I let loose the waterfall of nagging worry about my choice to jump a train all alone, it would be like confessing I've screwed up. So instead I crank up the volume on my music until I'm sure the woman next to me can hear the thumping through my headphones. I remind myself that fear never did anything to change the world. It only slows the process.

Even with the music rattling in my ears I keep imagining the scene unfolding back in Edenville. My grandmother Betty will have found my note by now. She'll have called my mother and the entire family has probably snapped into action. My police officer uncle Bobby is undoubtedly trying unsuccessfully to track my cell phone I turned off and pulled the battery from. My father will be barking at a bank teller to release information about the joint account he and I share. But there will be no clues there either; I moved most of the money to a new account last week. One he doesn't have access to. Their heads will be spinning with worry and anger, and every second will be torture. *For that I am sorry.*

The real problem is turning eighteen didn't magically make them see me as an adult. They didn't throw a party to welcome me to the club of grown-ups. They still picture me as the freckle-faced little girl who they need to shield from the world. But I've always felt ready to fly. I've just been waiting for them to open my cage and set me free into the world.

My family will have to deal with that. They'll have to find a way to understand I am not meant to spend my life in Edenville, or maybe not even North Carolina. The world is big and broken, and I want to see it without the cheery sanitized view through the filter my parents have provided. There is more waiting for me than quiet nights on my grandmother's porch. There has to be.

As trees rush by and the landscape around me changes from everything I've grown up watching to something I've never seen before, I can feel my courage finally outweighing my fear. I can do this. I have to ignore what my parents are afraid I can't do and remember what they've shown me I am capable of doing.

CONTINUE The Edenville Series with Book 3, <u>Stars in a Bottle</u>

Book 3: Not Just an Echo

The Clover Series:

Hearts of Clover - Novella & Book 2: (Half My Heart & Change My Heart)

Book 3: All My Heart

Over the Edge Series:

Book 1: Facing Home

Book 2: Crashing Down

Midnight Magic Series:

Amelia

Rough Waters Series:

Book 1: The Goodbye Storm

Book 2: The Runaway Storm

Book 3: The Rising Storm

Stand Alones:

Running From Shadows

Yours for the Taking

****

Multi-Author Series including books by Danielle Stewart

All are stand alone reads and can be enjoyed in any order.

Indigo Bay Series:

A multi-author sweet romance series

Sweet Dreams - Stacy Claflin

Sweet Matchmaker - Jean Oram

Sweet Sunrise - Kay Correll

Sweet Illusions - Jeanette Lewis

Sweet Regrets - Jennifer Peel

Sweet Rendezvous - Danielle Stewart

Short Holiday Stories in Indigo Bay:

A multi-author sweet romance series

Sweet Holiday Wishes - Melissa McClone

Sweet Holiday Surprise - Jean Oram

Sweet Holiday Memories - Kay Correll

Sweet Holiday Traditions - Danielle Stewart

Return to Christmas Falls Series:

A multi-author sweet romance series

Homecoming in Christmas Falls: Ciara Knight

Honeymoon for One in Christmas Falls: Jennifer Peel

Once Again in Christmas Falls: Becky Monson

Rumor has it in Christmas Falls: Melinda Curtis

Forever Yours in Christmas Falls: Susan Hatler

Love Notes in Christmas Falls: Beth Labonte

Finding the Truth in Christmas Falls: Danielle Stewart

****

BOOKS IN THE BARRINGTON BILLIONAIRE SYNCHRONIZED WORLD

By Ruth Cardello:

Always Mine

Stolen Kisses

Trade It All

Let It Burn

More Than Love

By Jeannette Winters:

One White Lie

Table For Two

You & Me Make Three

Virgin For The Fourth Time

His For Five Nights

After Six

Seven Guilty Pleasures

By Danielle Stewart:

Fierce Love

Wild Eyes

Crazy Nights

Loyal Hearts

Untamed Devotion

Stormy Attraction

Foolish Temptations

You can now download all Barrington Billionaire books by Danielle Stewart in a "Sweet" version. Enjoy the clean and wholesome version, same story without the spice. If you prefer the hotter version be sure to download the original. <u>The Sweet version still contains adult situations and relationships.</u>

Fierce Love - Sweet Version

Wild Eyes - Sweet Version

Crazy Nights - Sweet Version

Loyal Hearts - Sweet Version

Untamed Devotion - Sweet Version

Stormy Attraction - Sweet Version - Coming Soon

Foolish Temptations - Sweet Version - Coming Soon

NEWSLETTER SIGN-UP

If you'd like to stay up to date on the latest Danielle Stewart news visit www.authordaniellestewart.com and sign up for my newsletter.

One random newsletter subscriber will be chosen every month this year. The chosen subscriber will receive a $25 eGift Card! Sign up today.

AUTHOR CONTACT INFORMATION

Website: AuthorDanielleStewart.com
Email: AuthorDanielleStewart@Gmail.com
Facebook: facebook.com/AuthorDanielleStewart
Twitter: @DStewartAuthor

CPSIA information can be obtained
at www.ICGtesting.com
Printed in the USA
BVHW031143170419
545798BV00001B/6/P